WILD PITCH

CHICAGO COYOTES

DIAMOND WARRIORS

TL HAMILTON

TL HAMILTON

Wild Pitch

This book is a work of fiction. All names, characters, places, and incidents are the products of the author's imagination. Any resemblance to actual events, locales, or actual persons, living or dead, is entirely coincidental.

Cover Art © Clarise Tan @ CT Cover Creations 2026

Cover Photo © Lindee Robinson Photography

Editing: Kaye Kemp Book Polishing

TL Hamilton

10 9 8 7 6 5 4 3 2 1

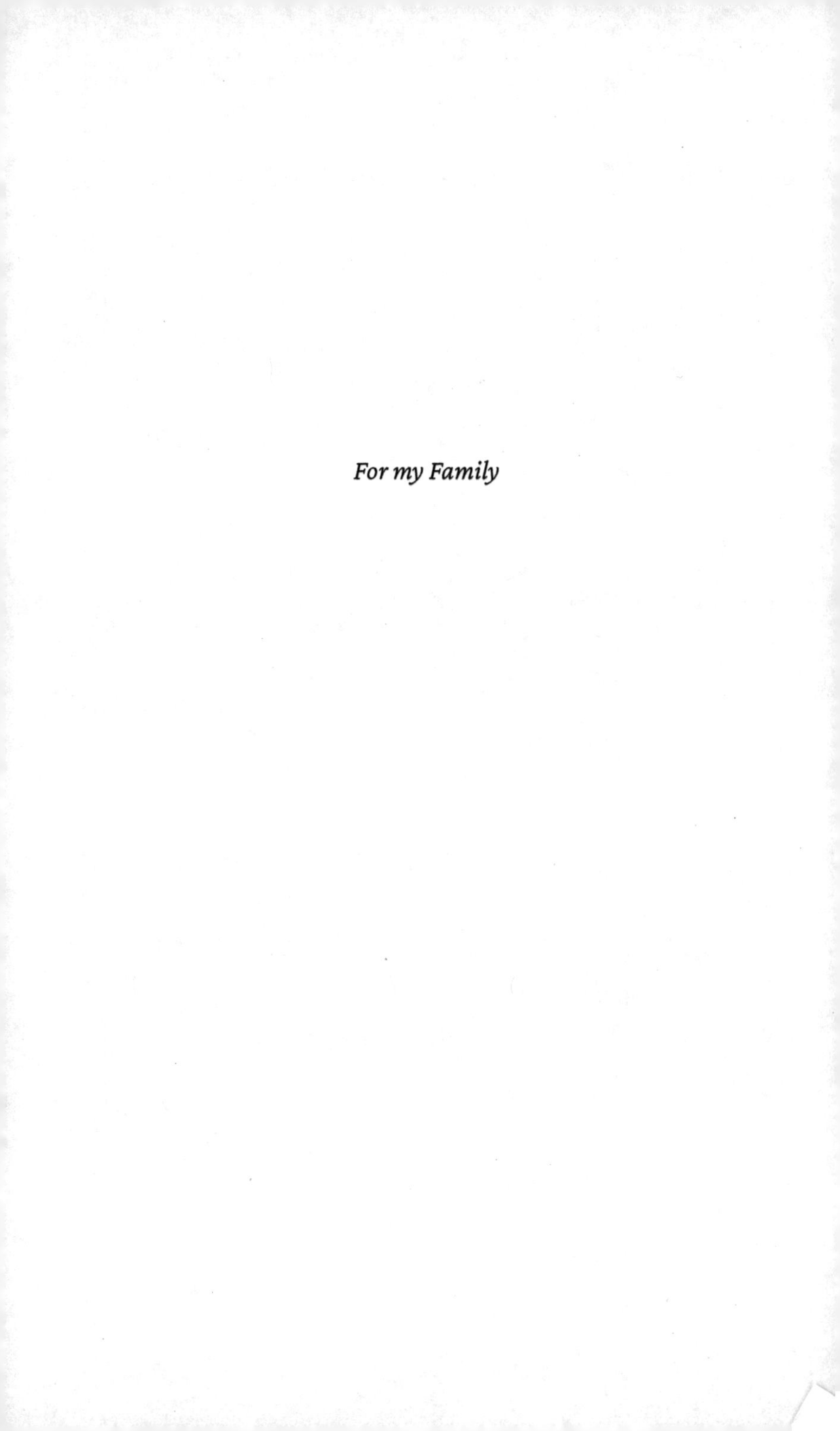

For my Family

WELCOME TO THE WORLD OF THE DIAMOND WARRIORS

Welcome to the Warrior Sports League world. The authors of the Warrior Sports League have teamed up to bring you professional sports romance stories filled with love, laughter, and heat–on and off the field.

What you need to know:

• While the cities featured are real, the **teams and players are purely fictional**.

• Each book will spotlight teams from across the series, but **they're not part of a single shared season**—so yes, you'll see **multiple champion teams** across different stories.

Get ready to fall for your next favorite player, and don't forget to join the official fan club of the Warrior Sports League on Facebook here: https://www.facebook.com/share/g/9e8NgrPn35epeRDH/

MEET THE DIAMOND WARRIORS

San Antonio Stars - Annelise Reynolds
Carolina Sunrays - Amy Stephens
Chicago Coyotes - TL Hamilton
Midland Magics - Haven Rose
New York Rebels - Heather Dahlgren
Salt Lake Rattlers - Rachelle Stevensen
Lexington Vipers - Michelle Savage
Charleston Water Dogs - Chelle C. Craze
St. Louis Snipers - Maria Vickers
Lake Tahoe Blues - Quinn Ryder
California Cougars - Kathleen Kelly
Roswell Comets - A.R. Hall
Seymour Lions - Jaime Russell
Racine Ravens - Melissa Filla
Greeley Raptors - Dawn Sullivan

DIAMOND WARRIORS SERIES PLAYLIST

Annelise Reynolds - Champion by Carry the Throne
A.R. Hall - Legend by The Score
Michelle Savage - Come with Me Now by Kongos
Amy Stephens - Diamond Eyes by Shinedown
TL Hamilton - Hall of Fame by The Script
Jaime Russell - Renegade by Styx
Chelle C. Craze - Batter Up - Nelly
Maria Vickers - Another One Bites the Dust by Queen
Haven Rose - Seven Nation Army by The White Stripes
Quinn Ryder - Blue - KNY Factory Remix Eiffel 65
Melissa Filla - Highway to Hell- AC/DC
Heather Dahlgren - Centerfield by John Fogerty
Dawn Sullivan - Bring That Fire by War & Hall
Kathleen Kelly - Thunderstruck by ACDC

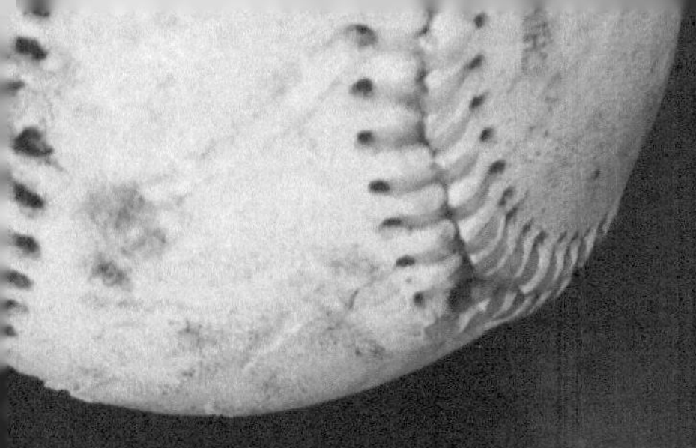

CHAPTER ONE

Cami

Trident Field was a Chicago institution. Every summer, baseball fans would come in droves to spend the day eating hot dogs, drinking beer, and cheering on the Chicago Coyotes.

Every kid in my third-grade class dreamed of stepping up to the plate and hitting a home run on those hallowed grounds.

I'd always been more interested in pitching a fastball that would crush all the little boys' dreams of glory.

Even in winter, the walls of the stadium cast long shadows in the morning sunlight, and the orange-and-black colors of the Coyotes were prominently displayed on snow-dusted banners leading up to the main entrance.

As I killed the ignition on my Volvo XC-40—a ridiculously expensive gift from my twin brother on our twenty-ninth birthday last year—it occurred to me that fate had a funny way of making your dreams come true while giving you nothing you ever expected.

The freshly plowed parking lot stretched behind me, dotted with the occasional car, but mostly empty. When the season started, those spaces would be filled with cars of every make and color. A sea of vehicles that weary, sun-stroked fans would have to navigate at the end of every game, while planning to arrive earlier the next week.

Coaching staff and management were already hard at work preparing for the upcoming season, and as of today, I would be too. So long as no one minded my tagalong.

"This is so cool. Will we get to go out on the field?" My niece, Zara, was a spitfire after my own heart. At ten years old, she was as sports-obsessed as anyone with the Morales name.

"*We* are going to do whatever my new bosses tell me to do," I said, giving her my best serious aunt look.

Her eyes lost none of their sparkle as she released her seatbelt and reached for the door handle.

"You still haven't told me why you aren't in school right now."

When Christian called this morning, I'd expected a *good luck on your first day*. A *we'll celebrate when I get home from this away game*. What I didn't expect was a panicked plea for babysitting and a knock on my front door before I could remind him that he wasn't the only one with work commitments.

Being the starting quarterback for the Chicago Engines football team meant that the work flexibility had been left out of his contract, and we were incredibly lucky that our found family were as supportive as they were, but sometimes schedules clashed, and I had to remind myself that I'd volunteered for the emergency care role. Had given up my professional sports career to move home and help my brother raise his daughter.

The very same daughter who was avoiding eye contact.

"Zara?"

"Okay, so here's the thing..." She flopped back in her seat, eyes trained on the ceiling. "Yesterday we had to do a presentation in class on what we wanted to be when we grew up. I said I wanted to be an athlete because...duh." She rolled her head toward me and raised a brow. I mirrored the expression because, for her, it *was* obvious. Her whole support network was made up of athletes, and she'd shown the same affinity for sports since she could walk.

"Anyway, it wasn't that big of a deal. Ms. Watson needs to touch grass."

"What wasn't a big deal?"

The clock was ticking, and I was painfully aware of the need to be on time, but sometimes being the responsible adult meant checking in on the well-being of your niece first.

"Bobby Knightly said I couldn't be an athlete." Her face screwed up as she fisted her hands in her lap. "He said that I should do something useful with my time so I could be a good wife someday. Learn to sew, or cook, or something." Her shoulders relaxed as a small smile played around the edge of her mouth.

"So I pitched a dictionary at his head." A giggle bubbled out of her. "It hit him right between the eyes, and his face... you should have seen it! I told him that I was clearly more athletic than him, so maybe he could learn to cook or sew instead. That's when I got sent to the principal's office."

Don't laugh. Don't laugh.

One of the hardest parts of being an adult was encouraging pro-social behavior when what I wanted to do was high-five her and take her for ice cream for putting the misogynistic little shit in his place.

"It's not our place to use violence to punish ignorance. Next time, just walk away. Okay?"

"But—"

"We need to get inside."

The reminder of where we were made her face light up as we hustled from the car and toward the main entrance.

"Do you think any of the players will be here today?" Zara's head was on a swivel as we passed the ticketing area and a deserted concession stand.

"I don't know. Probably not. They'll be preparing to fly out for preseason training."

"Will you introduce me to Smith Warren?"

I lengthened my stride to match my niece's frenzied pace. Like the idea of meeting her baseball idols was some kind of locomotive force that couldn't be contained, she charged through the halls without knowing her ultimate destination.

"Will you slow down? I don't think I'll have much to do with the designated hitters. Pitching coach, remember?"

"Oh, yeah. So can I meet Gage Wilson then? That'd be lit."

I caught her arm as she overshot the stairs and directed her upward.

Admittedly, I was trying to keep a lid on my own excitement. Like any Chicago-born athlete, I followed the home team, and with their current lineup, the Coyotes could take it all the way, if not this season, then definitely in the next couple of years. They'd taken time to build a team that was young enough to make a difference in the sport while other teams relied on their veterans to see them through. Gage Wilson was one of the best of his generation, but I'd seen areas for improvement in his game tape from the previous year, and I couldn't wait to get him out on the mound.

"Maybe in the future. For today, you're a fly on the wall."

Zara threw herself around the next corner, buzzing loudly. I chuckled, pulling up short as I came face to face with Zane Byers, head coach for the Chicago Coyotes, and my new boss.

"Hi, Coach," I said, trying to shuffle a red-faced Zara behind me.

"Morales, good to see you. I meant to meet you at the entrance but got held up. You find us okay?" He smiled widely, offering his hand, but I didn't miss the flash of disapproval in his eyes as he glanced Zara's way.

"No problems at all."

I returned his handshake and waited to see if he'd comment on Zara's presence. The team's public stance was family first, and I'd made it clear during the interview process that there may be times when I had to bring Zara to work with me. It wasn't ideal that I had to test the waters so soon, but I wouldn't apologize for it.

After a weighted moment in which I refused to break eye contact, he coughed and stepped aside, indicating the hallway behind him.

"Let me give you the tour."

Zara squealed and slapped me on the back, her enthusiasm dialed back up to eleven now that she knew she'd get to see every corner of the stadium.

The building was an architect's dream, with as much thought given to aesthetics as to practicalities. I knew from experience that the design had taken into account the easy ingress and egress of thousands of fans on game day, but I had never taken the time to consider the way the ceiling was angled to optimize acoustics, or the subtle detail in the molding that emphasized the grandiosity of the space. Coach Byers was a wealth of information, talking at length about the history of the building and the choices that led to Trident Stadium being one of the greatest examples of Chicago architecture in sport.

All thoughts of building design were left in the dust when we stepped out onto the field.

Was it possible the sun shone a little brighter as I pictured myself walking across the rich green grass up to that perfect mound of dirt with a ball in hand? Probably not, but the temptation to flop into the snow and create a snow angel like Zara had just done was a little overwhelming.

Lucky for my professionalism, my thirty-year-old joints didn't move quite the same anymore, and I refused to start my new career with the embarrassment of freezing my ass off on the ground when I couldn't spring back up.

"Pretty impressive, huh?" Coach Byers asked, a contented smile playing over his lips like he could see exactly what I could. This place was made for legendary acts.

"Come on. We've got one more stop before we head into the office."

He strode toward the exit as I herded a reluctant Zara after him.

"Can't I just stay a little longer? You can come pick me up later."

"Fly on the wall, remember? Let's move."

She huffed and dragged her feet as we stomped through the snow to where Coach Byers had stopped to talk to someone. The man was tall with dark hair that brushed his collar from where it stuck out from beneath an orange-and-black Coyotes beanie. He wore a tight Under Armour thermal shirt that showcased an impressive upper body. When he turned slightly, I caught a glimpse of a tidy beard and a strong jawline.

"Holy shit."

"Language," I chided, but Zara had already charged ahead.

She skidded to a stop in the snow and grinned as both men turned to stare.

Shit.

I hurried my pace, ready to run interference, and could have kicked myself when I realized who had Zara excited.

"Ah, Coach Morales. I was just telling Wilson here that you would be flying out with him tomorrow."

The news that I was flying interstate within twenty-four hours didn't land as hard as it probably should have as I mentally compared the face I'd seen countless times on the television screen, both in a professional capacity when preparing for today, and beforehand as an avid Coyotes fan, to the man before me. He was still stunningly attractive—as many news outlets and gossip columns would attest—but the subtle twist of his mouth, the slight scrunch of his nose like he'd detected an unsavory odor, were new.

It wasn't unusual for men in baseball to believe that women didn't belong in their sport. I felt a sinking sensation in my gut that one of my new players fell into that category. Instead of making myself small or cowering from the negative energy, I did what I did best.

Mentally told him to fuck himself and embraced my full feminine power.

"Absolutely, I can't wait to get into it. If you work hard,

we can fix that sorry excuse for a curveball you were throwing last season."

His gaze flicked to me for a second before he turned his back on me, delivering one word to Coach Byers before he strode away.

"No."

Like I didn't matter. Like he had any fucking say in what happened next. Without knowing a single thing about me as a person or as a coach, he dismissed me.

The snowball caught him directly in the back of the head. His shocked look mirrored my own as the cold seeped into my fingers.

What the fuck had I done? I was supposed to be professional. It was *not* professional to throw a snowball at one of your players on your first day on the job.

I should have apologized. Claimed a moment of insanity and prayed Coach Byers has a sense of humor. Straightening my shoulders, I took a deep breath.

"That's how you throw a proper curveball," I said, hoping like hell I hadn't just signed my own resignation papers.

Zara choked on a laugh.

Coach Byers cleared his throat, while Gage Wilson ran his palm over the back of his neck and flung snow onto the ground.

"I think we can end the tour here for today. I'll send you the flight details. Reach out if you have any questions, all right?"

I nodded, unable to break away from the stare-down with the pitcher I was going to have to find a way to get along with. It felt like a test. Like any chance I had of gaining his respect was wrapped up entirely in my ability to wait for him to break eye contact first.

It happened a moment later when he reached for his collar, like some ice had slipped down his back.

"You'd better not be late tomorrow," he grumbled, shrugging his shoulders with a grimace before stalking off the ground without a backward glance.

"You're cooked," Zara whispered as soon as Coach was out of hearing range.

I was a terrible role model.

"Let's get ice cream on the way home."

We wandered out of the stadium, and when my cell buzzed with an incoming email, I found all my flight and accommodation details ready for the following day.

I settled into my seat, and as the engine hummed to life, Zara made a small noise in her throat.

"You know, Aunt Cami, your throw was *almost* as good as mine."

Worst. Aunt. Ever.

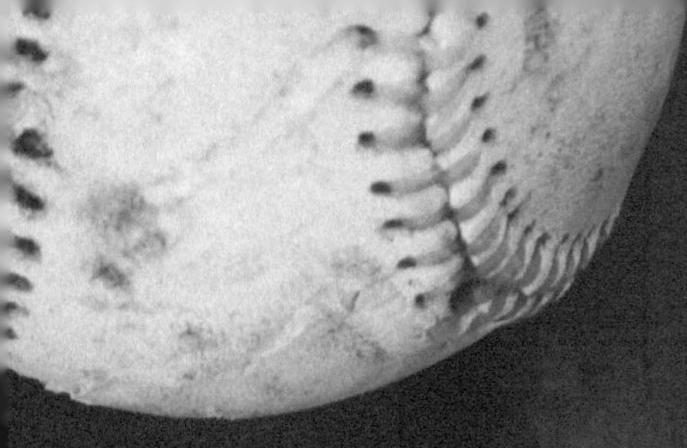

CHAPTER TWO

Gage

THE ARIZONA SUN beat down on my shoulders, a welcome reprieve from the icy snowscape I'd left behind. I loved Chicago for the culture. For the nightlife and the sports fans. There was no better place to call home, but my God, the winters were long, and preseason training was always a much-anticipated break from the February chill. If only I could bring my housemates with me.

"Can you put Nana on the phone? I just want to check on her. You know she gets anxious when I fly out."

I wasn't about to admit it was me who got anxious leaving both of them.

"You left us six hours ago. Do you think I've already managed to poison her?" My grandmother's voice was dry as the desert that was almost visible from my hotel balcony, but with a subtle warmth that reminded me why she was my favorite person in the world.

"I don't know...there was that time with the Hershey bar..."

"Oh, for goodness' sake. Will you ever let an old woman live down her lowest moments?"

I chuckled as a scraping came down the line, followed by happy panting.

The image of my giant, scraggly-haired beast of a Wolfhound brought a smile to my face. It had been love at first sight when I found her at the shelter, and she'd won my heart all over again when Gram melted for her.

"Hey, Nana girl. How are you doing with Grams? Are you being a good girl? I bet you are. You're the best girl."

There was a gentle whine, and then Gram returned.

"Her tail is wagging so hard I had to rescue my cup of tea. Now you've assured yourself we are safe and well, when are you heading to camp?"

"I should be heading out—"

A loud knock preceded our best closer, Chuck Bates, invading my hotel room.

"Now," I finished, sliding the balcony door closed behind me and holding a finger up at Chuck.

Gram chuckled and ended the call with an *I love you.*

Chuck bounced on the balls of his feet, red curls flopping in his eyes as he rolled a baseball between his hands. The guy was a ball of energy on his lowest day, but today something seemed to have him extra hyped.

"You ready to head out? I can't wait to meet our new coach. Apparently, she was pretty hot shit a few years ago. Nice to look at, too, from what I can tell of her pictures online."

Right.

Cami Morales had been a popular topic of conversation on the flight over, especially because we hadn't seen her on the plane. No one knew I'd met her the day before, and I had no intention of making it common knowledge. I suppressed a shiver at the phantom sensation of snow dripping down my back. What grown adult throws a fucking snowball?

Her. Apparently.

I didn't bother to respond, just grabbed my kit bag and headed for the elevator.

This season had to be my best yet. Focus on the prize and keep all other distractions at a distance. Much as I wanted nothing to do with our new pitching coach, she was right about my curveball. I'd let my personal life interfere with my performance far too much last season, and I had a lot to prove.

Chuck's babbling came to an abrupt halt as we stepped into the clubhouse, and I didn't have to look to know what had caused the shift. The energy of the other sixteen men who had made the journey for preseason training was all the same. A mix of anticipation and excitement for the upcoming season, with a heavy dose of respect and, in far too many cases, a dash of lust for our new coach.

She was a tiny thing, maybe five foot four or five, if I was being generous, with killer curves and a really fucking good arm. I'd flat-out refused to Google her like Chuck had, but her reputation still preceded her. Long dark hair hung from a tight ponytail beneath a Coyotes cap, brushing the small of her back as she turned toward the group of men loitering nearby.

"Welcome to preseason training, gentlemen. I'm Coach Morales. The next four weeks are going to be about making sure you are in the best condition to ensure the Coyotes bring home the Diamond League title this year. We're going to start things off right with a run to get the blood flowing, then head to the gym for strength and conditioning. Let's get going."

Forty minutes later, everyone's enthusiasm for our new coach seemed to have worn thin as she led us in a tight turn and up through the bleachers for another stair climb.

"Let's speed it up, gentlemen. My under-fifteen girls keep pace better than you. Push to the top."

There was a low grumble around me as my teammates complied with her demands.

"Now I know why she looks so damn tempting. She's the fucking devil," Chuck huffed as he caught me on the mezzanine level.

I grunted.

"Can you stop talking about how attractive you find her? You're going to find yourself in trouble with HR. She's our coach. Plus, she has a kid."

"What, you've never heard of a MILF? How do you know she has a kid? Been doing some of your own research?"

He poked my side like he was one of the women in my gram's knitting circle looking for gossip. I didn't have the time or, honestly, the breath left for this conversation, so I pushed ahead, ignoring the burn of my glutes as I finally hit the top of the fucking stairs.

"Good job. Straight down to the gym for strength training." Coach Morales clapped me on the shoulder as I passed by.

"The heat sure is something here, isn't it? I could go for a snowball about now." I didn't look at her as I said it, but I felt the tension in her fingers before she pulled her hand back.

"Listen..." The remorse on her face sent a flush of rage through me. It was too familiar. Too close to home.

"You can fuck off with your apology. Just be a professional, yeah? Can you manage that?"

Red crept up her throat, and her eyes narrowed. I held my breath, ready for what came next as she opened her mouth...and snapped it shut. A plastic smile stretched across her face as the next group of pitchers hit the top of the stairs.

"Great work, guys. We're heading to the gym next. Grab some water on your way through."

Something sank in my gut as my red-faced teammates murmured words of respect and funneled past. I turned away before she could catch my eye, rubbing my stomach and wondering if the yoghurt I had for breakfast had been past expiration.

Because there was no way I was disappointed that she didn't give me a mouthful for being a shit to her.

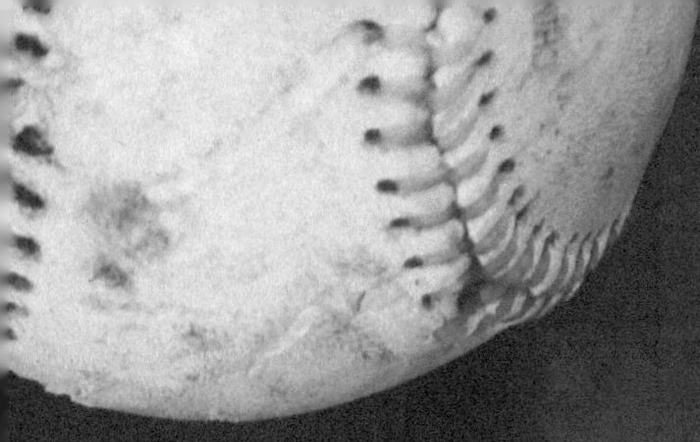

CHAPTER THREE

Cami

After eight weeks of preseason training, I'd learned a number of things about myself and the Coyotes as a team.

Chuck Bates was an unapologetic flirt who froze up if he received any hint of returned interest.

Becoming a pitching coach was both the best and worst decision I'd ever made.

And Gage Wilson was the world's biggest pain in the ass. If I told him to work on strength training, I'd find him pitching practice balls for the catchers. If I sent him to run sprints, he'd decide to visit the physio. We'd had more than one closed-door argument where he seemed to derive pleasure from being torn a new one. He was either trying to systematically destroy my sanity, or he was a masochist.

Possibly both.

"Sorry I'm late." Alina Wynters, head journalist for the women's sports magazine, *Fierce*, slid into the seat opposite me with a tired smile. Her blonde curls circled her head in a riot of disarray, and the dark smudges under her eyes spoke of sleepless nights with the baby she'd had four months ago.

When she first reached out with the idea of a piece about my return to professional baseball, my first instinct had been to turn it down. I couldn't imagine anyone being interested in a pitcher who retired a decade ago and moved into the coaching space, but when she mentioned how my return to professional sports had inspired her to get back into the career she loved, and how many women shared the struggle of finding themselves after raising children, I found it difficult to say no.

I felt like a fraud, though. Yes, I'd left my career behind to help Christian raise Zara after her mother left them, but maybe I'd already been looking for the door before I got my brother's call.

"Can I get you a coffee?" Alina asked, waving to catch the attention of a server.

I smiled at the young server who bounced over wearing a Mabel's Bakehouse T-shirt, an enthusiastic grin, and a name tag that said 'Bomb'.

I loved coming here. Not only did they make the best apple danishes in Chicago, but the staff were all underprivileged kids who were given training in customer service and food preparation to help them find future employment. The bakehouse often ran trivia nights where proceeds went to local charities, and at the end of each day, unsold produce went to the food bank on the next block.

"What can I get for you?" Bomb asked, hugging her tablet close to her body, stylus poised to take notes.

"The largest coffee you have and a tiramisu," Alina said, throwing me a sheepish look.

"Make that two coffees and an apple danish. I get

hangry when I go too long without one." I stage whispered the last part to Bomb, and Alina's shoulders relaxed.

During the football season in Zara's early days, when I took over the primary parenting role so my brother could keep a roof over their heads, I had been perpetually late. I'd plan to be somewhere on the hour and find myself elbow-deep in a diaper change at five minutes past, often having no idea what day of the week it was. I remembered the sense of having a hundred balls in the air with the fear that they would all come crashing down and shatter around me in irreparable ways.

I still felt like that sometimes.

So when Alina slipped her laptop out of her bag and set up, apologizing again for her tardiness, I waved it off.

"When Zara was eighteen months old, I promised to take her to one of Christian's games because he misses her so much during the season. I was so worried about getting there late that I overcompensated."

Alina raised a brow.

"Two. Days. Early. I was so tired, I didn't even question why there was no traffic. It wasn't until I had her in the stroller and noticed the lack of crowds that I checked my calendar."

Alina laughed. "Oh, God. I hear that. I found my phone in the microwave last night. The only thing I can think is that when I heated up a frozen dinner, I put my phone in so I'd have a spare hand."

"It gets easier," I promised.

Although...did it? I'd stepped further and further back into the aunt role as Zara grew, especially when our support network expanded to include Marina and Weston.

Weston was the Chicago Engines' tight end and Christian's best friend. He was great with Zara and often stepped up to help with care for her where he could; plus he did the single best thing for our family when he introduced us to his neighbor.

Marina was an Australian psychologist who'd moved to Chicago with her daughter, Amber, after losing her husband.

Amber and Zara had been inseparable since the moment they met, and we'd built a found family that kept growing. First, when we adopted Ridley into our friendship group, then more recently Gia, Weston's new wife.

A glass shattered, and behind the counter Bomb bounced backward. "I'm okay."

"I love this place," I murmured, letting go of the memories as Bomb swept up the breakage, the tinkle of glass on linoleum and the brush of the broom barely audible in the quiet bakehouse.

Alina sat back in her seat, eyeing me closely as the veil of professionalism fell over her features. "So what has it been like running preseason as the first ever female on the Coyotes coaching staff?"

Nerve-wracking.

Full of imposter syndrome flare-ups.

The best thing I'd ever done.

"There's been an adjustment period, but all in all, it's been great."

"When you say *adjustment period*, do you feel there has been any resistance to you moving into the role? You've stepped into a league that has been notoriously sexist. How has the team adjusted, and what accommodations, if any, have you had to make to appease egos?"

It was a good question, and something I'd worried about more than once in the time between receiving the offer and taking the plane to Arizona, but other than Gage Wilson's belligerence, I hadn't had any overt opposition.

"I don't make accommodations for male egos. They can step up and prove they belong on the team under my coaching, or they can find another team to play on. We're not in the twentieth century anymore, and I've found that anyone who does have a problem with my gender will generally keep their mouth shut after a couple of hours of training."

I leaned across the table, lowering my voice like I was sharing a secret.

"I've heard grumbles that I'm a sadist when it comes to training."

Alina barked a laugh, smothering it with a hand as Bomb delivered our caffeine and sugar.

"Good to hear you're representing," she said, taking a long draw on her mug.

"Someone's gotta do it, and I need to set a good example for my niece. It won't be long before she's navigating the world of professional sports, and I want her to know she's capable of achieving anything with hard work."

We settled into an easy back and forth, discussing women in professional sport as a whole, the power of strong role models for the next generation, and the challenges women face trying to find life balance. Finally, Alina asked the question I'd been dreading. The one that should be easy to answer but came with complications.

"You're so passionate about women in sport and being able to do it all. What made you step back from your own career ten years ago? Why has it taken you so long to get back into baseball?"

"I've always been around baseball," I hedged. I wasn't

ready for the sporting world to know everything about me, apparently.

"I left the women's league when my niece was born because my family needed me. Christian had just been recruited to the Engines as quarterback, and Zara's mother wasn't in the picture, so at that stage of life, it felt like the time to prioritize family."

"Are you saying that your brother's career was more important than yours? You still hold records for pitching that others can't get near."

The danish sat heavy in my stomach as I considered the journalist in front of me. Gone was the tired mother who was running on caffeine and hopes of a full night's sleep some time in the next calendar year. In her place sat the professional who could walk into any magazine and be handed five figures for a story she hadn't yet written.

"As you said, I felt like I'd accomplished a lot in my short time in the professional league. It wasn't about putting Christian's career before mine, though as his twin, I always want to see him do well, but I was ready for a new challenge. I've been coaching girl's teams for as long as Zara could hold a bat, and I couldn't be more proud of the little sportswoman she's growing into. Now felt like the right time to step into the professional league because we have a support system that can help us maintain our work/life balance."

My shoulder twinged, a phantom punishment for the details I held back. Giving it a subtle roll, I sat back in my seat, ready to be done with the interview. Alina closed her laptop and gulped the last of her coffee.

"Thank you so much for your time today. I'll send through a final draft before we publish, if you'd like?"

“Please,” I said, pushing out of my chair and walking with her to the front of the shop.

“Thanks for coming. See you next time.” Bomb waved happily from behind the espresso machine.

I raised a hand at her as I ducked through the door and almost tripped over a monster. The thing was almost as big as me, with wiry hair that made it look like some kind of a demon horse. It pushed into my space, pinning me against the door jamb as I looked around desperately for help.

“Get away.” I pushed at its face, gagging at the breath that wafted out of its grizzled mouth. Instead of listening, it pushed closer, and I shuddered at the wiry brush of its fur.

“Nana. Heel.”

Oh, God. I knew that voice.

Between one breath and the next, I was free. The beast sat on the sidewalk, tongue lolling out of its mouth, beside the man I’d come to think of as my nemesis.

When Christian and I were young, our abuela—God rest her soul—told us stories of angels and demons. The lesson I learned well was that Lucifer wasn’t ugly or misshapen, but a beautiful angel, fallen from heaven for his sins.

Gage Wilson was my own personal Lucifer.

In gray track pants and a skin-tight thermal shirt, he looked like a sports lover’s fantasy. His ballcap was backward, covering his freshly shorn hair while highlighting his high cheekbones covered in light stubble.

“Fancy meeting you here, Coach,” he said, the sneer barely audible as he glanced between Alina and me.

“Gage Wilson, meet Alina Wynters. She writes for—”

“*Fierce* magazine. I’ve read your work. So you’re writing a piece on our lovely Coach Morales?” He wrapped an arm around my shoulder as Alina flushed.

I could understand the appeal, but how could she miss the evil twinkle in his eye? He was up to something.

As inconspicuously as possible, I tried to sever the contact between us. His grip tightened.

"I followed her career when she played pro herself. Who wouldn't take the chance to find out more of the story if given the chance?" Alina glanced at me, as though unsure how I would take the comment.

"A journalist is always going to be curious. Hopefully, my story is all you were hoping for." I tried again to slide away, but Gage wasn't having it.

Faking a cough, I flicked him in the crotch, then slipped free as he squeaked and flinched away.

You didn't grow up with a male twin without learning a thing or two about self defense.

"Well, it was lovely catching up, but I really need to get going."

I offered Alina my hand to shake and strode off toward my car without making eye contact with Gage.

Whatever he was up to, I wanted nothing to do with it.

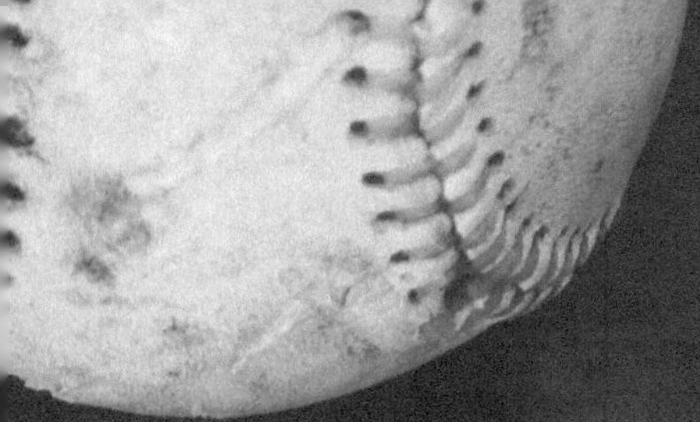

CHAPTER FOUR

Texts from the Ride or Die chat

Cami: SOS. Who wants to help bury a body?

Ridley: Who's dead?

Gia: I'm on set, but can bring a shovel in 2 hours

Marina: Is this individual already a corpse? Or just someone we dislike?

Marina: Don't answer that if it's the first one

Marina: Cami…did you kill someone?

Cami: No…but I can't promise I won't.

Cami: He's just the worst. He doesn't listen. He always says the worst thing at the worst time. He makes me so mad. He's just…

Ridley: The worst?

Cami: Exactly!

Marina: Cami…I have bad news.

Cami: What?

Marina: Is there any chance you're attracted to this guy?

Cami: *middle finger*

Ridley: He's hot. I just Googled him.

Gia: Who's hot? Damn it, they're calling my scene. Stop being interesting for a few, ok?

Cami: *middle finger* We're always interesting.

Marina: Boys suck

Cami: ??

Marina: He sounds mean

Cami: Amber?

Marina: No…I'm mum. Not Amber.

Ridley: *laughing emoji*

Cami: Where's your mom? You're too young for boy talk, though I appreciate the support. Boys do suck.

Ridley: Only if you find a good one

Marina: Sorry, I'm back. Amber doesn't need to hear about what boys do. But I'd like to know what the actual plan is for your pitcher, Cami. Isn't he really good? Otherwise you could try to trade him.

Cami: He's good, but he isn't teachable, so I don't know that he'll ever be as great as he could be. They won't trade him because he's the best on the team.

Ridley: *cough* best in the league

Marina: Shame.

Cami: Can you teach me to do that mind manipulation stuff you therapists do to make people do what you want them to? We can brainwash him into doing my bidding.

Marina: ...

Marina: Do you actually want me to answer that?

Cami: Sigh. No.

Cami: Unless we really could do it.

Marina: How about you work on building trust in your professional relationship and see if you can appeal to his sense of sportsmanship. Failing that, prove to him that he'll be able to win more. Men like winning.

Cami: This sounds like a Christian pep talk. Is he there?

Marina: No. But maybe I've spent too much time with him lately.

Cami: *shudder* be careful. There's no coming back from over-exposure to my brother

Marina: Don't worry, I'm immune.

Ridley: *coughs*

Cami: OK, fine. I'll play nice. But I expect a girl's night out soon as a reward.

Marina: We'll go to a nightclub so you can threaten bodily harm to any man who approaches our group

Cami: I love that you get me

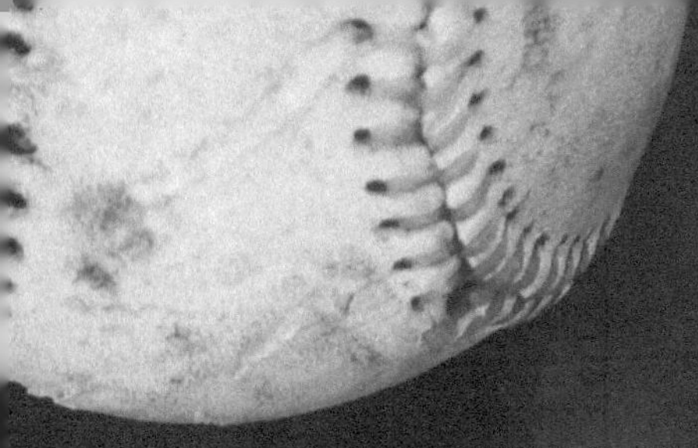

CHAPTER FIVE

Gage

The California sun beat down on my shoulders as I strode toward the mound on the Cougars' home field. The warmth bleeding through my shirt did nothing to relax me as a certain pitching coach nagged me with her eyes from the dugout.

Get in the zone.

I'd spent the morning warming up in the bullpen with Chuck, working the muscles in my shoulder and arm until they hummed with energy, ready to strike out every one of the Cougars. Coach Morales had been there for almost as long with 'helpful' feedback.

You haven't warmed up properly.

You're over-reliant on fastballs. Work on your curveball.

Stop ignoring the warning signs. You're overworking your arm.

Was she right? Maybe. But what I did was working for me, so I had no intention of changing what wasn't broken.

Stepping up onto the mound, I allowed myself a moment to absorb the roar of the crowd. The scent of dirt and sunscreen on the warm breeze. In my hand, the ball was a familiar, solid mass that I knew would find Bailey's glove where he crouched behind the plate.

I lived for these moments.

We came out strong, and it was now the bottom of the first inning and up to me to keep the Cougars from putting runs on the board.

Shuffling my feet on the plate, I waited for Bailey's signal to come through.

"Four seam fastball," the speaker in my hat chirped, and I smothered a grin.

Hell yeah. Let's start this thing strong.

I wound up and sent the ball straight down the line, my shoulder burning with the power of the throw.

Strike one.

Bailey tossed the ball back, and we fell into a familiar pattern of back and forth, some pitches landing perfectly in his glove while occasionally catching an unlucky break that had loaded up the first two bases.

A flash of green and gold edged into my peripheral vision as I wound up, and before they could backtrack, I sent the ball flying toward Warren on second, who sent the player back to their bench. Second out. The crowd lit up with a combination of applause and boos, nicely balanced, considering we were the visiting team.

Bailey called a curveball for the next play.

Try again.

Splitter.

Let's go.

I struck out the next batter and headed off the field to prepare for the next inning.

"Wilson." Her voice cut through the corridor as I headed back toward the locker room after the game.

We'd won by a tight margin, but a win was a win, and all I wanted to do was grab the headphones I'd forgotten and head back to my hotel room. She called my name a second time, but I kept moving. I'd found the best way to deal with Coach Morales was to take her direction as more of a suggestion. It had nothing to do with the joy I took from seeing her eyes light up with fury. Couldn't have been that her searing words and abrasive attitude made me...trust her. Maybe even like her.

No. Not like.

She was the one woman I never had to guess where I stood because she'd tell me. At length. And volume.

She looked soft and sweet from a distance, which fucked with my head and put me in a bad mood, but she was a firecracker of a woman who was endlessly entertaining when riled.

"Gage Wilson, stop right now. Why the fuck are you incapable of following the most simple direction? Do you get off on pissing me off?"

I wasn't going to answer that because the truth was...maybe?

Her brown eyes were almost glowing with rage as I spared her half a glance before continuing into the locker rooms.

This was dangerous. Coaches were to be respected. She had the power to bench me for the season. She could get in Coach Byers's ear and insist he trade me for someone more compliant.

I was one player, and she was the first-ever female coach for Chicago.

Didn't stop me closing the door in her face.

And that didn't stop her from barging straight in after me.

Nothing about our surroundings registered as she closed the distance between us. Not the rows of lockers that had held our neatly pressed jerseys with our numbers clearly displayed before the game. Not the table in the middle of the room with chairs left askew from Chuck clowning around while we all rode the winning high as we changed after the game.

My attention was solely, dangerously focused on the woman who came so close that I could smell the amber-and-lily scent of her shampoo. She tilted her chin up, and even though she barely reached my shoulder, she managed to suck all the air out of the room. A part of me resented her for it.

"Just because you blew off my debrief doesn't mean you get to avoid feedback you need to hear. You're avoiding pitches I know you can make and overusing fastballs. It's making you predictable. Worse, you're going to injure your shoulder if you aren't careful."

A big part of me wanted to ask why she cared, but even I wasn't belligerent enough to voice such an obvious question. She was my coach, and the team relied on my arm to be game ready.

A chunk of hair had slipped loose beneath her ball cap. I wondered if it was as soft as it looked. As she moved her head, the giant hoop earrings she insisted on wearing swung in and out of view from behind the curtain. Her throat was pink, whether from frustration or sunburn, I couldn't tell. The urge to see the flush of color spread rode me as I opened my mouth and stuck my foot in it.

"You think I haven't noticed your fucked-up shoulder? You're not perfect. I've got this handled." No one had mentioned an injury, and Google had been a bust when I *hadn't* spent a sleepless night researching my coach. Really. But the way she unconsciously rotated it at the end of a day of training, coupled with how she protected it when she was demonstrating another fucking curveball technique, led me to believe that she herself may have had a bad habit or two on the mound.

There it was. The flush crept into her cheeks, her chest heaving as she stepped into my personal space. "How the fuck do you think I hurt it in the first place, you egotistical, blow hard, son of a bitch?"

I couldn't say what happened next.

Her proximity. The smell of her skin. The fire in her eyes.

I blacked out.

The next thing I was aware of, my arm was wrapped around a soft body. My other hand fisted in her hair, which had come entirely loose from my rough handling. Her lips tasted like cherry. The noise that left my throat was pure hunger as I swiped my tongue across the seam of her mouth.

Let me in.

This was what I needed. This connection. It had been too long for both of us, and as she opened beneath my questing tongue, I didn't hesitate to dive into her sweetness. Home.

The kiss heated up quickly as she met me with a force that was unlike the Peyton I knew so well. She was timid and sweet. A gentle presence that wanted to keep everyone happy...well...until she didn't. Anger surged, and I tightened my grip as new memories surfaced. Tears and apologies, and an empty house, which meant...

Reality crashed into me in an instant. This wasn't Peyton. This was...

Crack.

I flinched at the burning in my cheek and dropped my hold on Coach Morales.

"What the fuck was that?" she asked, holding the back of her wrist to her lips like she was too shocked to wipe my kiss away.

A fine tremor shook the fingers on her hand as she shuffled from foot to foot. Her eyes, however, burned through me like they knew exactly where my mind had gone.

To throw her off the scent, I forced a smirk. "You have a hell of an arm, Coach."

She blinked, and her whole body relaxed. I both hated and loved that snark and deflection was a language we shared.

"What are you, some kind of masochist?" she asked.

Footsteps echoed outside the locker room door, and we froze until they continued past. The visiting team locker room was not the place to be kissing my new coach. What the hell had I been thinking?

"I guess I am," I agreed, running a self-conscious hand over the back of my head. "Or maybe I was just giving you another opportunity to touch my dick. You seemed to enjoy it the first time. Are you always that forward, Ms Morales?"

Her jaw dropped. "I did not touch your dick."

"Oh, yes, you did. I have witnesses."

Her eyes dropped to my crotch, and I didn't bother to hide my smile.

"Okay, firstly, I was defending myself, not trying to touch your...anything." She brushed past me and paused with her hand on the door. "Besides, there wasn't all that much to touch."

A laugh broke from my chest as the door swung shut behind her.

"Liar," I called, grinning like a madman.

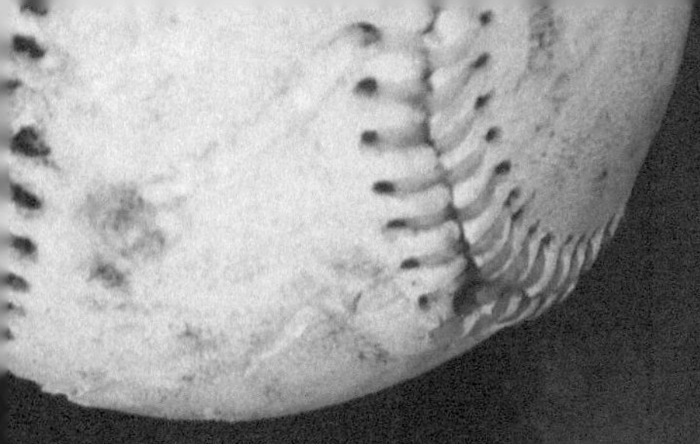

CHAPTER SIX

Cami

Sweat dripped down my spine as I strode toward Coach Byers's office. Each strike of my heel brought up a new and unwelcome image. Dark locker room. Angry words flowing unimpeded from my mouth. His arms wrapped around me. Then hot skin. Warm breath. Arousal.

No. Not arousal.

Fury.

At him. At myself. I was a professional, damn it. Coaches didn't go around kissing their players. There were rules about that kind of thing.

I had to come clean.

The smiling faces of coaches and players from years gone by seemed to close in on me as I hurried my steps.

We know what you did. You don't belong here, they whispered in my head.

Stupid, misogynistic players. *He* kissed *me*. I wanted to shout.

"What the hell do you know, with your stupid, smiling faces, anyway?"

"Morales?"

Coach Byers leaned out of his office door, brow furrowed as his eyes flicked between me and the photo he'd just caught me bitching at.

I took a deliberate step away from the wall and wiped my palms over my sweats.

Run away. Maybe he didn't notice anything unusual.

"Hey, Coach, I'm glad I caught you. Do you have a second?"

Please say no. You're too busy. Far more important things to worry about than...

"Sure, come on in."

Damn.

The head coach's office was sparsely decorated, but homey. A heavy wooden desk sat at one end of the room, with an old school desktop computer in one corner and a baseball signed by Bobby Miller—one of the greatest pitchers the Coyotes had ever produced—in a glass case on the other. There were no personal effects in the room, and it occurred to me that I knew very little about Coach Byers's personal life. Was he married? Did he have kids? A dog? Or a fish?

Taking up a large portion of the wall space to my right was a TV screen that was playing highlights from the Lexington Vipers vs. Greely Raptors game. Lush, overstuffed leather chairs dotted the space, providing areas to sit with varying degrees of formality. Two chairs and a coffee table could be used for a casual chat, while the ones in front of his desk could be for a more professional discussion...or reprimand.

Coach threw me a smile as he crossed the room, and I

watched his bright white Nike sneakers disappear behind the desk as he settled into his chair and gestured to the seat across from him.

When Christian and I were twelve, we stole a cake our mom had made for a bake sale. Neither of us particularly liked fruitcake, but when a dare was laid down, we both refused to flinch. We ate the entire thing in one sitting, cringing at every mouthful, and daring the other to back down until there was nothing but a pile of crumbs. Christian went off to football practice with a stomachache, while I was forced to make the cake again from scratch.

The sense of shame I felt back then for having to bear a punishment for a crime I didn't want to commit in the first place reared its head now as I met Coach Byers's stare.

"Gage Wilson kissed me after the game in California."

The clock on the wall continued to tick.

My knee bounced triple-time as the temperature soared in his office.

His face didn't change. No flinch. No surprise registered. Nothing.

"Go on." His voice was as difficult to read as his features. Was he pissed? He was probably pissed. Maybe he couldn't say much because he was busy writing up my termination papers in his head.

"Well..."

Was I really just going to throw Gage under the bus? We'd both participated in the breach of rules. God. Should I have brought Gage with me for this talk? It would have severely impacted my efforts to avoid him, but maybe it would have been more professional.

Maybe the best I could do was tell the whole truth and hope for the best.

"I followed him into the locker rooms to yell at him

after the game and then we kissed. Oh, and then I slapped him so...yeah. I guess that's it."

He leaned across the desk and steepled his fingers. "Are you reporting him for sexual misconduct, or yourself for physical assault?"

"Ahhhh...neither?"

"Is that a question?"

"No?"

This was getting more uncomfortable by the second. Maybe it would have been easier if he did fire my ass because this back and forth was making me nauseous.

He scrubbed his hands over his face and sat back in his chair, the small movement making it seem like a chasm of open air had opened up between us. This was it. The punishment for doing something I didn't want in the first place coming to land.

"Cami, are you here to declare a relationship with a player?"

"Fuck no. I hate fruit cake."

His brow furrowed, mouth opening slightly before he shook his head. "Then let's call this a learning moment and get on with the season. Thank you for keeping me informed. Now get out of my office and back to your job."

I stumbled to my feet, feeling like I'd made a last-minute catch on a fastball headed for my face. The unsteadiness continued as I made my way through the clubhouse and found the team relaxing in the cafeteria.

"Coach!" Bates bounced over, grinning like a kid. "Gage's gram made pastries. Come and grab one before they disappear."

I let him tow me toward a group of players who were all crowding one of the long tables. The players moved aside, muttering words of greeting as we approached. It occurred to me that there was respect in their voices. The way they made room, even in their recreational space. What the hell had I been thinking putting this at risk by kissing...

"Pastry, Coach?" Wilson's eyes held the hint of a challenge as he pushed a half-empty box of heavenly looking danishes toward me.

"There's apricot, cherry and—"

"Apple," I said, snatching one up before he could rescind the offer. For good measure, I took a couple of steps back so I could ensure I was out of reach before taking a bite.

At this point in my life, I considered myself somewhat of a danish connoisseur. I'd eaten them in every major city I'd ever been to, and twice when I visited Germany. I'd tried the ones made with red apples instead of green (green was superior), I'd tried the ones that included golden raisins (why did people want to mess with the perfect apple texture?), and, on occasion, I'd had the holy grail of danishes. The ones that were so perfectly balanced they could send you into a gastronomic trance where the world melted away and there was nothing but you and the sweet perfection of flaky pastry and stewed apples seasoned to perfection.

"I think she's drooling."

The comment snapped me out of my moment of happiness, and I turned my best glare on the man who was both the provider and interrupter of joy.

"It's time to get moving. Everyone, out on the field. We're going to run suicides for the next twenty minutes."

Groans erupted from the players around me, and Bailey knocked his shoulder into Wilson on his way past. "Dude, don't piss off the coach. She's going to punish all of us because you can't help being a dick to her."

"You'll survive," he replied, sending me a smirk that made the temperature in the room soar.

Was there a problem with the heating in this place? Or maybe I was going into early perimenopause.

It was possible.

As soon as the last player left the room, I returned my attention to my pastry and enjoyed the hell out of every. Single. Bite.

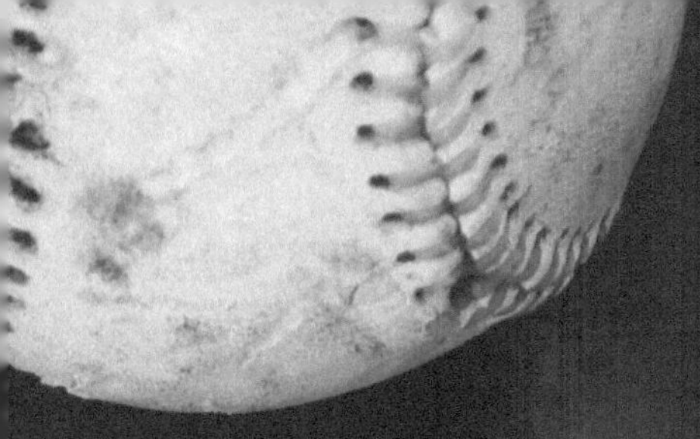

CHAPTER SEVEN

Gage

"Gram, your pastries were popular today," I called as I stepped through the front door.

The click of nails on the hardwood floor preceded Nana's entrance from the kitchen. She never rushed, my Irish Wolfhound. Every move was considered. She was like the Dalai Lama of dogs.

"Hey Nana girl, where's Gram at? Have you been a good girl for her?"

Nana's long, pink tongue lolled out of the side of her hairy muzzle as she gave me a big doggy grin. Those impossibly kind eyes shone with a love I'd never doubted under this roof with my two favorite beings in the world.

"Gram?" I called, gently guiding Nana out of my path and moving farther into the house.

The kitchen was empty, though the scent of yeast lay heavy in the air and a fresh loaf of sourdough cooled on the counter. I checked the sunroom next, but our knitting projects lay abandoned where we had left them the day before. A pitcher of lemonade sat on a side table, condensation beading the jug, with two tall glasses positioned beside it, ready for our afternoon get together. She had prepared for me to be home, so I knew she couldn't have gone far. My gram loved rituals, and she'd said on many occasions that our afternoon knitting sessions were her favorite time of day.

A buzzing broke into my thoughts, and I pulled out my phone, wondering who could be calling. The name on the screen was the last one I was expecting, and as I had exactly zero intention of answering the call, I left the device beside the lemonade, just barely resisting the urge to let it go for a swim.

The garden.

Gram had been told by her doctor that she needed to slow down. That with her arthritis advancing, she needed to let me take over the manual labor in the house and practice self-care to avoid flare ups. Gram had responded in no uncertain terms that manual labor was self-care. That she was perfectly capable of looking after herself and her grandson, and that he could pry her gardening shears from her cold, dead hands. The doctor had laughed. Gram had laughed. I'd broken out in a cold sweat, imagining those hands.

Gram had been my hero for most of my life.

When my parents abandoned me so they could travel the world and live carefree, she'd given me a loving home with routine and the stability I needed to thrive. When they returned and tried to take over my life after I signed my first contact with the Diamond League, she'd told them to take a hike and ensured they could never take a penny from me. She'd lived a mostly solitary life since my grandfather passed when she was pregnant with my father but hadn't thought twice about taking on a runt of a kid who had a chip on his shoulder and aggression in his veins.

Because of her, I channeled those feelings of inadequacy into a pitching arm that was the best in the league and made myself into a man who wasn't afraid to go after what I wanted. Granted, I probably hadn't been showing my best side to my new coach, but I got a sick kind of enjoyment out of seeing her fire up.

"Nana, where's Gram?"

I let the dog wander ahead of me as we wandered through the maze of rose bushes that marked the start of a garden that could have been on the cover of a magazine. I'd had journalists ask to do just that in the past, but I liked my privacy, and the last thing I wanted was to make my gram into some kind of sideshow for baseball fans to speculate over.

A small knot formed in my stomach as we turned into the orchard and still couldn't see any sign of life.

"Gram?"

She hadn't left home. Her car was parked at the side of the house, where it always was. The faded green AMC Gremlin, a relic I'd asked repeatedly to update for her, but could only convince her to let me service. It had been my grandfather's, and sentimental value was the only form of currency that mattered to my gram.

A soft whine came from behind the herb garden, and my breath froze in my lungs as I found Nana sitting beside the prone form of my gram.

"Shit. Gram!" I skidded across the ground on my knees like I was sliding into home, reaching for my phone to call for help.

I cursed again as I pictured the device on the table in the

sunroom and kicked myself for leaving it behind. Who gave a shit about my problems when Gram needed help?

As gently as I could, I rolled her onto her back and checked for a pulse the way I'd learned in the First-Aid course we'd taken together during the offseason a couple of years ago. I'd told Gram it was a good skill to have at the time, all the while praying I'd never have to use it to help her. This was my worst nightmare come to life.

The soft, wrinkled skin of her throat felt too delicate as I searched for signs she was all right. I couldn't lose her. I wasn't that strong.

"Gage?" Her tiny hand wrapped around my fingers, and I blew out a hard breath as her eyes fluttered open.

"What happened? You scared the fuck out of me, Gram."

"Language," she chided, attempting to sit up.

"I got you."

Before she could protest, I swept her into my arms and strode back toward the house. She was so light. The force of nature I'd known my entire life felt as heavy as an empty bat bag in my arms. Her face was milk-white beneath her neatly styled hair, still in perfect condition despite her impromptu grass nap.

"You can put me down, boy. I just got a little dizzy. I'm fine now, really."

I ignored her protests until we stepped through the door of the sunroom, and I deposited her on her chair.

"I'm fine."

The glass of lemonade wasn't as cold as I would have liked, but I handed it to her anyway, refusing to move until she'd drunk the entire thing.

Next, I called her doctor and confirmed we could come in for a checkup in an hour.

"You're fussing for nothing, Gage. You have better things to do."

"Nothing is more important than you. I'm not leaving your side until you get the all-clear from the doctor."

Like fate had nothing better to do than test me, my phone buzzed with an incoming call from Coach Morales.

"Answer your phone. I could do with a break from your hovering."

She loved me, really.

I didn't want to leave her completely alone, but with the mood I was currently in, I didn't want her to hear how this conversation could go.

Stepping just outside the door, I wandered down the first row of roses until I was out of earshot but still had a line of sight to where she sat slumped in her chair.

"Coach Morales, long time no see. Did you miss me?"

The words were sharp, an invitation to the back and forth neither of us seemed to be able to resist.

Right on cue, she blew out an agitated breath, and my shoulders dropped some of their tension.

"Training tomorrow morning at seven. Don't be late."

"I need my beauty sleep, Coach. Seven seems like an ungodly hour. Maybe you should reschedule until after I've had my physiotherapy session at nine."

Movement in the sunroom caught my attention, but I relaxed as Gram poured herself another glass of warm lemonade and sat back in her chair.

"Seven sharp, or I'll reshuffle the pitching order for the Vipers game this weekend."

We both knew she was bluffing, but considering I was also bullshitting, I let myself enjoy the moment.

"Have fun explaining to management how we lost the game due to your reshuffle," I teased.

"Fuck, you're an arrogant son of a bitch. Why can't you just say *yes, coach* and leave it at that?"

The answer was because her ire was grounding me in the wake of a situation that left me feeling really fucking untethered.

But since I couldn't say that, I gave her the closest thing to truth I could.

"I have a lot of shit going on, so I'll see you when I get there tomorrow."

The cursing coming through the phone as I hung up made me smile, and I headed back toward the house a little lighter.

Of course I'd be at the stadium on time. Gram had instilled a strong work ethic in me that included the need to be early to everything.

Not that Coach Morales needed to know that. I'd let her sweat about it overnight.

The idea of being on her mind did not give me a sick sense of pleasure.

Not at all.

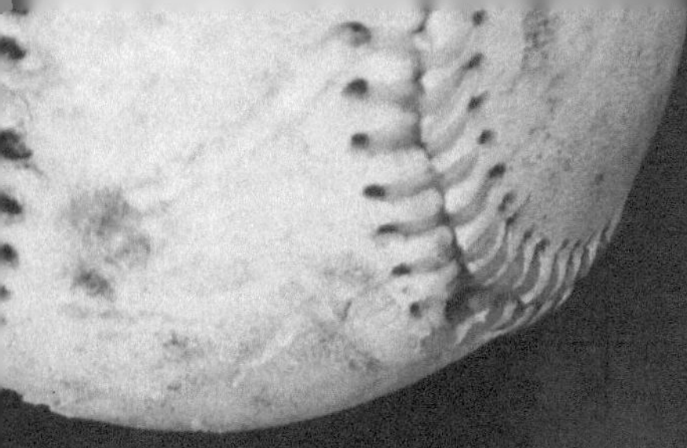

CHAPTER EIGHT

Cami

"Any questions?" Coach Byers cast a quick glance around the coaching staff, and no one made a sound as I cast another subtle glance at the door. I had Zara in tow today since Christian had been volun-told by his PR team that he had a closed photoshoot for an undisclosed brand endorsement. He'd been told in no uncertain terms that a teacher development day was no excuse to have a child on the shoot, and to be flexible with all timings.

The result of this was a very early morning wake-up call along with a healthy dose of anxiety after leaving Zara sitting on a bench outside the meeting room for over an hour while I attended the game day coach's meeting. David, our batting coach, shifted in his seat, and I telepathically threatened to kick him in the balls if he dragged the meeting out any longer. Whether my psychic acuity had improved over the years or, more likely, my resting bitch face was on point, he dropped his eyes and waited until we were dismissed to approach Coach Byers for whatever was on his mind.

I hustled out the door, planning on where I could safely stow Zara while I ran tape for my pitchers, and pulled up short at the sight of a very empty bench in the hall.

Where the hell had she gone?

Aside from my workmates, who were slowly filtering out of the meeting room and toward the cafeteria down the hall on the right, there was no one else around.

Figuring she might have gone looking for lunch, I followed the crowd.

"Has anyone seen a little girl?" I asked over the noise of the players seated at the long tables.

Aside from a couple blank looks, the talking and banter continued, but it was clear Zara hadn't come this way by the relaxed atmosphere and lack of a small, dark-haired girl talking the players' ears off.

Had she gone looking for a restroom? I checked every women's restroom in the clubhouse and promised myself I wasn't going to panic as each new place turned up no sign of my wayward niece.

Christian, you had a good run. I just thought you'd like to go out on a high, and ten years of parenting felt like a good place to leave it.

As much as my brother's superstition rivaled that of a hockey player's, and the idea of finishing well was right out of his playbook, I didn't think he'd buy the argument when it came to his daughter.

Where the hell could she have gotten to?

The rec room was clear. So was the media room and Coach Byers's office.

"If I were a ten-year-old girl, where would I be?"

The answer came to me like a lightning bolt, and I took off at a run.

Through the halls and past Coach Byers's office, out the front door of the clubhouse and toward the diamond.

The crack of a bat meeting ball, followed by a squeal of delight, slowed my steps, and I'd mostly managed to lower my blood pressure until I caught sight of who my niece had talked into a little batting practice.

"Great hit. Did your mom teach you to bat?" His body moved with an ease that seemed criminally unfair for his size as he retrieved the ball. The orange-and-black design of his Coyotes T-shirt perfectly displayed rounded shoulders and biceps that would look bitable on a man who wasn't one of my damn players.

"I don't have a mom."

My heart clenched at the dismissive note in her voice. It wasn't fair that Zara had been left without a mother. The selfish bitch was top of the list of people I'd smite the fuck out of if I ever got superpowers.

"I don't have a mom either." Gage's voice carried easily to me, despite his soft tone, and I wondered how much more I had to learn about my most infuriating pitcher.

"Do you have a dad?" Zara asked, lowering her bat.

I should have made myself known to them. Standing at the edge of the dugout, I felt like a voyeur, looking in on a bonding moment that was none of my business.

Gage shook his head, tossing the ball between his hands.

He was an orphan? Shit. Now I felt bad for yelling at him all the time. Wasn't it a thing that people were morally obligated to be nice to orphans?

Okay, so maybe I was kidding myself that I could be really nice to him, but maybe I could lay off a little.

"My mom and dad left me with my gram when I was little, maybe a bit younger than you. But it's okay, because my gram is awesome."

"Oh, my mom left too. So now it's just me and my dad. And Aunt Cami, and Weston, and Gia, and Ridley, and Marina, and Amber. Amber's my best friend even though she doesn't love baseball like I do, but we both love football, so that's all right."

Gage chuckled, and something stirred low in my gut. Especially as he squatted to Zara's level and met her eye.

"It sounds like you have an amazing family. They've certainly done a great job raising you, even if your loyalties are divided between baseball and football. Maybe I can convince you there's only one true sport if you keep working at your batting."

Zara laughed, and I smothered a smile as she gave his shoulder a condescending pat. "My dad would never let that happen, but good luck trying."

Gage frowned, and I hustled out from behind the dugout.

"Why would your dad—Wait. Morales. Is your dad—"

"There you are! Zara, what have I told you about running off?"

"I didn't run off. Gage offered to pitch some balls for me to work on my swing." She turned her back on the player and widened her eyes in an emphatic plea for understanding. "Gage offered to pitch for me."

I understood exactly what she meant. If I had been offered the opportunity to bat with a Diamond League star pitcher at her age, I would have forgotten my entire family history to make it happen. Screw Christian and his football schedules. Forget about what Mom had planned for the day.

None of it would have mattered.

It didn't make it any easier being the concerned adult, though.

"You should have waited for me," I said instead, eyeing the adult who was responsible for this mess.

"Zara, you can use the cages to keep practicing your hitting, if you want. I'm going to have a quick chat with Gage."

"But—"

"No buts. You're in my bad books right now, so go practice. You have a game coming up soon too, and at your level, you still need to have good batting form to play."

With a dramatic sigh, she retrieved her bat and slouched her way across the field like it was a burden to be able to use the multi-million-dollar facilities for her practice.

As soon as she was out of earshot, I turned toward the one person I could actually vent my anxiety on.

"Come with me," I growled at the hesitant look in my pitcher's eye.

How dare he abduct my niece without a word of warning?

Had he taken her to fuck with me? He was supposed to be in the gym this morning. *Not that he looks like he's missed the session*, my mind whispered, giving me an inconvenient reminder of how nicely his shirt stretched out across the back of his shoulders.

And the way he overshared about his home life? So unprofessional. It was like he wanted to find things in common with Zara.

Like he was trying to relate to her. Make her feel normal.

It wasn't his place to be kind to her.

But he'd done it anyway. He'd gone out of his way to make her feel welcome in the stadium, then shared a part of himself to make her feel okay because he wasn't sure if he'd messed up by mentioning her mom.

Despite the fact he didn't know Zara, and didn't like me, he'd still given her his time. I stepped down into the dugout and waited for him to follow, desperately trying to find the indignation that had driven this talk in the first place.

"I'm sorry," he said, holding his hands out like he could physically suppress the dressing down he expected.

I took two steps toward him, then surprised the shit out of myself by pulling his mouth down to mine. His grunt told me neither of us had expected this turn of events, but he caught up quickly, scooping his arms beneath my butt and pushing my back into the side of the dugout.

What the fuck was I doing?!

The thought drifted away like a balloon on a clear day as his tongue licked at the seam of my mouth, demanding entrance. I opened to him, tasting mint on his breath as he sighed against my lips. His big body surrounded me as the kiss intensified, his little noises of encouragement adding fuel to the fire of urgency as I felt him harden against my sweats. I whimpered, tightening my legs around his hips as pleasure zinged through my body.

"Fuck yes," he breathed, digging his fingers into my ass cheeks as he tilted his hips, chasing the sounds that I couldn't keep in.

I wasn't a prude when it came to sex. I'd had my fair share of bedmates over the years, but as my body flushed with a familiar warmth, it occurred to me that it had been too long since I'd been intimate with anyone.

Surely deprivation was the only reason I found myself

pinned to the wall by a man I was pretty sure I still hated and on the verge of orgasm.

A small whimper escaped as Gage broke the kiss and dropped his head into the crook of my neck.

“Come for me,” he muttered against my skin, the warm breath setting me off, even as my brain screamed I’d gone too far.

I bit his shoulder, trying to suppress the scream that wanted to escape me as I shuddered my way through a really fucking good orgasm. I didn’t want it to be good. I wanted him to be mediocre, but as he tightened his grip and his breath left him in a stutter, I found cold consolation in the fact that at least we were both fucked.

And at least I didn’t have a wet patch on my pants to show for it.

As soon as he stilled, I pushed at his shoulders until he dropped me so I could make sure that was true.

All clear.

And time to go.

“Hey, wait.”

I ignored him as I walked back onto the field, subtly checking my clothes were all in order.

“Cami, wait a minute. Aren’t we going to talk about this?”

I kept walking, throwing back over my shoulder, “You’re late for your gym session. Maybe stop by the equipment room and pick up some new sweats first, then go do your shoulder workout.”

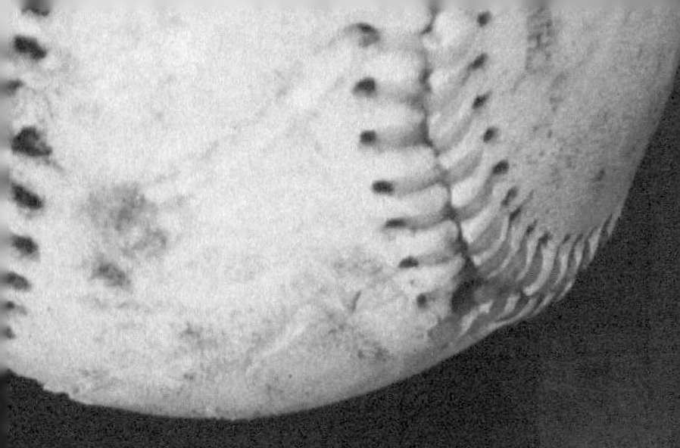

CHAPTER NINE

Gage

What the fuck had just happened?

I stood in the dugout for several long minutes, cum cooling in my boxers as I tried to make sense of the morning. I'd had a shit sleep, even after the doctor gave Gram the all clear. He'd ruled that it was probably a case of low blood sugar because while she spent a lot of the day baking, she often forgot to feed herself any of the things she made. I'd wanted to yell at her for not taking care of herself, but even the thought of it made me feel like a shitty human being, so I'd gone in to work out at five a.m. and ran into the little girl when I stopped for a snack break.

Zara. I'd almost walked straight past her on her seat outside the briefing room, but when she called my name, I recognized her from the first day I met her…aunt. She had looked so similar to Coach Morales I hadn't questioned any of her motives until we were already on the field. I hadn't been lying when I said she was a good hitter. For being ten years old, she already showed a lot of signs of being a great athlete. It wasn't a surprise, given who her father was. How had I not realized that Coach Cami Morales was related to Christian Morales, star quarterback for the Chicago Engines? Probably because I was too busy staring at her ass.

My palm tingled, thinking about how perfectly it had fit in my hand.

Had the last twenty minutes really happened? Or did someone slip me a psychedelic, and while I was happily living out a fantasy where I got to make my coach come, my body was sprawled on the ground somewhere beneath the stadium. Maybe being transported to an undisclosed location to be used for nefarious purposes.

I pinched myself and cursed, rubbing away the sting. Did that mean it was real? I shifted on my feet and grimaced as the stickiness in my pants convinced me I was safe from abduction, but not from the embarrassment of coming in my pants if anyone caught me in my current condition.

A shower was definitely needed. Decision made, I beelined for the clubhouse, praying I didn't run into anyone between here and the showers.

It turned out someone up there had to be listening, because other than some slight chafing, I made it to my destination without incident.

The shower was deliciously warm as it beat down on my back, and I took the opportunity to replay the moment in the dugout when, instead of chewing my ass out like I'd expected, seeing as I had technically run off with her niece while neglecting her training plan, she'd shoved her tongue down my throat and rubbed up on me until we both came.

It was fucking glorious.

I wanted it to happen again.

The problem was, I had no idea how things had taken that turn. My analytical mind played the tape forward and backward, searching for that point, seeking a way to replicate the situation and coming up with nothing except the fact that women were mysterious and unpredictable. The cynical part of me scoffed. We'd already learnt that lesson. No need for a repeat.

But that, more than anything, was what I liked about Cami Morales. She didn't leave you guessing or try to sugarcoat anything. She was unapologetically herself.

From her soft skin to her sassy mouth, she drew you in and burned you in the best possible way.

Without conscious thought, I worked my fist over my growing erection, shamelessly reflecting on the way her eyes lit up with ire when I went against her plans or questioned her decisions.

Fuck, maybe I was a masochist.

I imagined the water running over my aching cock was her mouth, reprimanding me for thinking about her in such an unprofessional way while sucking me deep into her throat. My lower back cramped as I tightened my grip to the point of pain, imagining her digging her nails into my ass as she came, but this time I was inside her, forcing her to take more pleasure than she could have imagined.

I came with a yell loud enough to echo through the cavernous shower room, and as awareness crept back in, I prayed no one had finished their workout early. Toweling off quickly, I slipped into my clothes and smothered a curse as Chuck looked up from his locker with a smug smirk. Apparently, my luck had run out.

"Gotta release the pressure sometimes. I get it. But if you didn't wash down the walls afterward, I'm gonna have to kick your butt."

My first impulse was to insist that of course I'd cleaned up with myself, but the glint in his eye told me he was still fucking with me, so I pushed past without defending my hygiene habits, because at the end of the day I had been caught jerking off in the clubhouse showers.

Thank God I hadn't said her name out loud.

I paused, the blood draining from my head in a rush. Fuck. Had I said her name?

My phone rang as I pulled into my driveway, and a part of me perked up at the idea it could be Coach Morales calling to discuss what happened this morning.

No points for guessing which part.

Regardless, it sank like a stone the second I saw the caller ID.

Why the hell was *she* calling again? I'd said all I had to say to her eight months ago, and that was one memory lane I had no intention of strolling back down.

Mindful of the mistake I'd made the night before, leaving my phone out of reach when Gram needed me, I rejected the call and pocketed the phone before I retrieved my bag from the backseat of my car and headed inside.

"Dinner will be ready in fifteen minutes. Go wash up." The familiar greeting made me smile, and instead of complying, I wandered into the kitchen in time to see Gram pull an entire roast leg of lamb out of the oven.

"How many people are you planning on feeding?" I asked, closing the oven for her and moving a wooden board to the counter for her to drop the pan on.

"You're a growing boy, and this will give us cold cuts for

the rest of the week. I worry about you getting enough to eat during the season. You always look so thin by playoffs."

She cupped my cheek, sharp eyes scrutinizing me like she could see the weight dropping off as we spoke.

"I'm definitely not still growing, but the fitness plan during the season is brutal. Thank you for looking out for me." I dropped a kiss on her cheek. "Now what can I do? You sit down and let me wait on you for a change."

I was doing some studying of my own. Her face, while not as deathly pale as the day before, still looked a little gray around the edges, and I'd seen the tremor in her hand when she lifted the roast onto the counter. Gram wasn't exactly a spring chicken, but I hadn't previously been as acutely aware of her age as I had been over the last twenty-four hours.

"Stop your fussing. You've been working all day. Now go and make yourself presentable for dinner while the meat rests. I'll pour myself a drink and take a seat in a minute."

Rather than stress her out with an argument, I rushed through a quick shower and changed into some loose sweats and a T-shirt before rejoining her in the kitchen.

"Be a dear and carve the meat," Gram ordered, waving a pair of tongs in my general direction whilst dishing perfectly roasted potatoes onto two plates. Without hesitation, I complied, piling thin slices high on a platter for Gram to serve.

"Peyton called the house today looking for you," Gram said casually, retrieving two sets of cutlery from the drawer.

"Neither of us has anything left to say to her. If she calls again, just hang up."

Gram tsked. "I taught you better than that."

"I deserve better than her, Gram. I'm not the one who fu-messed everything up. I'm happier now, anyway."

Gram held an overloaded plate out toward me, watching me through narrowed eyes.

"You do seem happier today. What happened?"

"Nothing." The answer was too quick, and I mentally cursed myself as I accepted the plate and avoided eye contact.

"Gage Matthew Wilson, have you met a girl?"

Don't look her in the eye, or she'll read your mind.

Gram had always had an uncanny ability to tell what was going on with me, but I couldn't imagine her approving of me engaging in a lust/hate physical relationship with my coach.

"Let's just eat, shall we? This looks delicious."

She harrumphed, sinking into her seat as she temporarily let go of her impulse to find me a *nice girl to settle down with.*

When everything went down with Peyton, a good part of my anger had been at the fact that she had upset my gram. That alone was reason enough to never speak to her again.

Let alone everything else.

I dug into my meat and potatoes, the delicious meal tasting like dust on my tongue as I resisted falling into my spiraling thoughts.

And wished I could go back to the dugout with the mean woman who told me the truth.

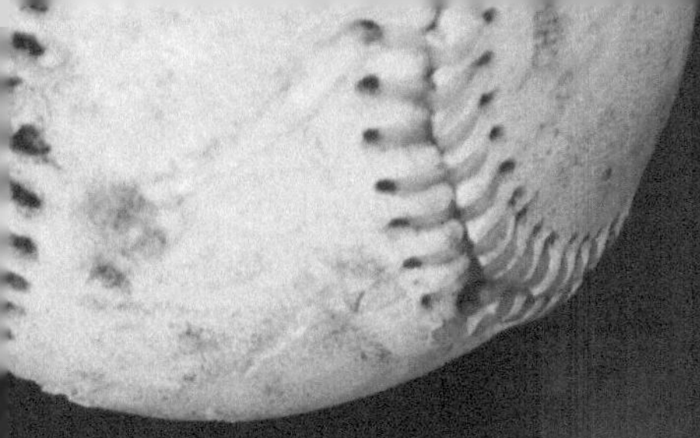

CHAPTER TEN

Cami

"Coach?"

Coach Byers glanced up from his computer screen, his furrowed brow smoothing out as he waved me in.

"Come take a load off, Morales. Unless you're going to report yourself for kissing a player again."

I paused halfway to the offered seat.

"Um..."

"Cami, did you kiss Wilson again?"

"I believe the correct term is frottage?"

I cringed as Coach Byers scrubbed his hands over his face with a sigh.

"Okay. First, I did not need that image in my head. I see enough of the player's shit in the tabloids without hearing first-hand accounts from my staff members. And second, are you here to declare a relationship?"

"No, I—"

"You hate fruitcake?"

What was he...? Oh. Right.

Note to self. Coach Byers had a great memory, and apparently, it extended to childhood guilt-related non sequiturs.

"Right," I said, finally sinking into the chair across from him.

"You're a great coach, Morales. I know there's a lot of talk about you being a publicity stunt, or a DEI hire, or whatever other bullshit armchair warriors like to spout because running their mouth is the only thing they've ever committed to practicing on a regular basis, but aside from whatever the hell is going on between you and Wilson, you've made the transition from player to coach pretty damn seamlessly. The players look at you with a healthy mix of fear and respect, and our strikeout rate so far this season has seen an improvement over this time last year.

If this is all some game in self-sabotage, then I'm going to have to ask you to leave this club out of it. Otherwise, stop letting Wilson get in your head and feel free to keep your personal life personal unless you suddenly acquire a taste for...fruitcake."

An inconvenient fantasy of me tasting Gage's fruitcake flashed through my mind, and I pushed it away before the embarrassment showed on my face. That was never going to happen, because I'd decided I would never be alone with Gage Wilson again.

Safety in numbers and all that.

"I will. Thanks Coach."

Taking that as my cue to leave, I hustled out of his office, wondering if he had a point about the self-sabotage. Was I intentionally trying to undermine myself? My shoulder gave a judgmental twinge, and I refused to rub away the pain as I went in search of my players.

The sound of my name made me pause at the door to the player's lounge, and I silently cursed as my resolution to avoid being alone with this particular man came crashing down.

"Do you have a minute?"

He inclined his head toward the media room, and despite my best judgment, I followed him inside, some small residual amount of good sense making me leave the door wide open behind us.

"What do you need, Wilson?" I crossed my arms and leaned a hip against the table, going for relaxed and aloof while feeling really fucking awkward. Mentally measuring the space between us, I took a casual step back and nearly slid off the edge of the table.

His hand came up in an aborted attempt to catch me as I found my footing, and we both froze.

His eyes were a darker brown in the dim light of the media room. In the sunlight, they were a golden caramel brown. Not that I spent a whole lot of time looking at his eyes. They were just...there. On his face. When he was doing things to deliberately piss me off.

His tongue darted out, wetting his thick lower lip, and I wondered if he'd taste like mint if I got close enough right now.

Bad, Cami.

"Please don't look at me like that. Half the team is on the other side of that door, and even that knowledge isn't enough to stop me thinking about what I'd like to do."

I blinked, coming out of whatever spell he'd put me under. Stupid athlete magic.

"I'm not looking at you like anything. Just over here wondering why you're wasting my time when we should be getting to work."

A muscle in his cheek ticked, and he gave me a small nod. There. Professionalism restored.

"Right," he said, rubbing his palm over the back of his neck and blowing out a breath. "I, ah...I just wanted to let you know I'll need a couple of hours off this afternoon. I'll make up the time later, but there's somewhere I need to be, and I can't reschedule it."

"So you want me to reshuffle my entire schedule to suit you?"

Damn it. He smelled really good. Like leather, fresh grass, and bad decisions. He was close enough now that I could smell the mint on his breath, and I bit the inside of my cheek to keep from leaning in and inhaling. He'd done this on purpose. Olfactory hypnosis so he can run his own routine. It was a thing; I was sure of it.

"Not your whole routine...I can practice by myself. Or just do an extra gym session, or something."

I shook my head, trying to clear my thoughts, and something like panic flashed across his face. Whatever he had to do, it was clearly important to him.

"What time do you need to go?" I asked with a sigh, eyeing the door.

He gave me a three-hour window in the middle of the afternoon which would only have impacted an hour of training, but I wasn't going to let him think he could have special treatment.

"Fine. We'll meet back here at seven p.m. Be ready to do any pitching drills I tell you to do."

This could work in my favor. He couldn't disregard my instructions in a one-on-one session. I could force him to work on pitching weaknesses.

Feeling a lot better about how things were working out,

I left him to whatever errands he had to run and headed out to train the rest of my team.

~

"So your solution to avoiding this player that you hate was to organize a special after-hours training session. Am I understanding this right?"

I used to like hanging out with my twin, but since we'd made friends with a psychologist whose daughter was now best friends with Zara, Christian had started making insightful observations that I didn't need to hear or acknowledge. So instead of doing either, I changed the subject.

"How was the shoot?"

Christian grunted, picking up Zara's mitt and ball.

"Long. They don't want me telling anyone about the sponsorship until it launches. The secrecy is bullshit. It's not like it's some left-field collaboration that will shock the masses. A sports-based brand is collaborating with an athlete. Shock, horror."

I snorted. My brother was the only person in Chicago who didn't know he was a big deal. He'd always just been unapologetically Christian, which was probably part of the reason I hadn't grown to resent the hell out of him, even though I'd lived in his shadow since we were kids.

"Where's Zara?" I asked, swiveling on my stool to follow him as he moved around the lounge picking up various pieces of sports equipment from Zara's after-school activities and his duffle bag, which had a habit of exploding over whatever room in the house he left it in.

"She went home with Weston to hang out with Amber. Apparently, Gia has a girl's afternoon planned for them."

"And you didn't want to tag along? Maybe spend some time with Marina?"

The back of his neck flushed a dark red as he straightened the cushions on the sofa. Our other friends may not have noticed, but I knew my brother well, and he'd had a hard-on for our Australian friend since the day they first met. I hoped he'd work up the courage to tell her how he felt, but until he did, it was my God-given right as his twin to give him hell for it.

"Maybe I can take her shopping for some new bras and panties. Do you want to drive us? You can wait in the cuck... I mean...husband chair while we try things on in the changing rooms."

He shot me a glare that was out of my playbook, and I returned the look with my best innocent smile.

"I've told you before, that smile makes you look constipated. And there's no universe where I want to be near you trying on bras and panties. Gross. Actually, the thought is making me nauseous." He coughed, feigning a dry heave as he moved toward me.

"Don't. No. Christian, I swear to God, I'll kick you in the balls." I held up my hands as he moved into my personal space, retching and heaving like the big, lumbering asshole he was.

"Seriously. Fuck off. How old are you, five?" I kicked him in the stomach, and he finally backed off, laughing like a damn hyena as he rubbed his abs.

Maybe it was better that Marina didn't know this freak was into her.

"I hate you," I muttered, straightening myself on the stool and trying to look composed. The bastard knew I couldn't handle vomit, so it was his go-to when he wanted to torment me.

It wasn't my fault I was an empath at heart. Beneath my bitchy, standoffish exterior was a sympathy vomiter.

No one—and I mean, no one—knew that about me except Christian. I'd made him swear he'd never tell a soul when we were ten years old, and he'd kept that oath, even if he still used it against me in private.

"So, Coach Byers said something weird to me today," I said, not sure why I was bringing it up at all.

"What's that?" he asked, settling into the stool beside me and pulling his coffee cup across the counter toward him.

"He suggested that whatever this is with Wilson might be self-sabotage. Weird, right?"

"Oh, it absolutely is." While my mouth dropped open, he gave me his best smirk and took a casual sip from his mug.

"What else would you call messing around with a player you claim not to like?"

"A bad decision?"

"Come on. You're smarter than that."

I sighed. "In my defense, he was being nice to Zara."

"Wait a minute. Are you telling me you screwed around with a player *in front* of my daughter?!"

"No! Of course not. She was in the batting cages."

Christian gave me a bombastic side-eye as he took a longer draw on his coffee.

"You're supposed to be on my side, you know," I griped, checking my mug to see if it had magically refilled. Nope, still empty. I sighed and slid off my stool to get the coffeepot.

"I am on your side, Cam. That's why I don't sugarcoat shit. It's the first time you've been in the pros in a decade, and I know you don't want to talk about what happened last time, but I'm worried you're going to do what you always do and deny yourself the chance at what you really want."

I slammed the pot on the counter a little harder than necessary, and lukewarm coffee sloshed over my hand.

"Damn it." I reached for a towel to wipe my hand and the counter. "What do you mean, *do what I always do*?"

"I don't want to fight."

"We're not fighting. Just having a discussion about how you think I sabotage myself."

If my voice was getting louder, it was just so he could hear me properly from up there on his high horse. I worked my ass off to get where I was. Harder than he'd ever worked for anything. Not because he hadn't worked hard, but being male and naturally gifted had made him a shoo-in for the pros since he was old enough to hold a ball.

"What happened ten years ago?" Rather than matching my heat, his voice got softer. And didn't that piss me off even more.

"Ten years ago? Stephanie left you and Zara to fend for yourselves. You seem to have forgotten that I gave up my career for you. And now you want to rewrite the story and say I sabotaged it myself? Fuck you, Christian. Nice gratitude you got there."

The second the words left my mouth, guilt crash-landed in my gut. It wasn't Christian's fault, or Zara's, that Stephanie was a raging selfish bitch who didn't realize she was walking away from the best people in the world because she felt the urge to 'find herself' when she should have been a mother to her newborn child.

Christian's face whitened. He dropped his gaze to his coffee and didn't move for a long minute.

"I'll never be able to repay you for the help you gave us

when we needed you," he whispered. "But I also know that your stats had been down that season. Since you injured your shoulder. You started playing it safe on the mound, and I think you psyched yourself out. Be mad at me if you need to, but maybe it's time to look in the mirror and decide if you want to keep the things you earn. Stop burning your bridges. You deserve everything and more, and I think sometimes that scares the shit out of you."

My next mouthful of coffee coated my tongue with bitter ash.

For someone who had known me our entire lives, he'd missed the mark on this one completely.

"I have to go."

Without waiting for his reply, I dropped my mug in the sink and strode out of his house.

I had work to do.

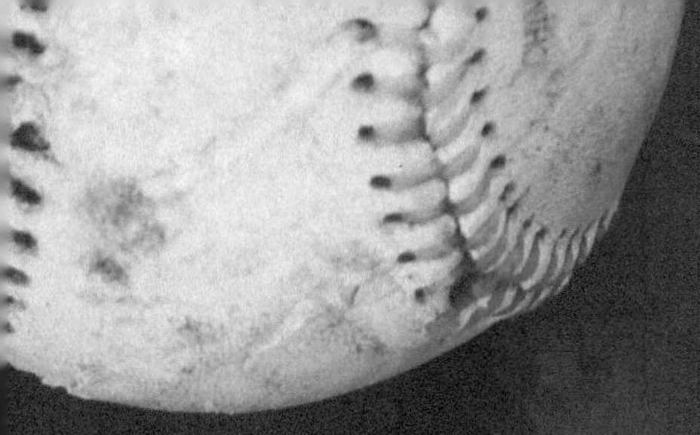

CHAPTER ELEVEN

Gage

Gram's blood tests had come back with an anomaly.

When the doctor called her into his office and insisted he could fit her in on the same day, alarm bells had rung in my brain. If there wasn't anything to be concerned about, he would have just waited for her next checkup the following week. Instead, I'd taken the afternoon off training to drive her despite her protests that she was quite capable of driving herself.

My head filled with images of her losing consciousness halfway to her appointment, crashing into a fire hydrant, and perishing in a ball of fire that preceded her car flooding and drowning her burnt corpse.

It was uncomfortably in line with how my luck had been going for the last twelve months.

Or for my entire life, really. I sometimes wondered if I'd made some deal with a devil in a past life where I would be eternally unlucky in life in exchange for killing it on the pitcher's mound.

Maybe one day I'd hear the howl of hellhounds, and my soul would be dragged to eternal damnation.

Or maybe I shouldn't have fallen asleep comfort-watching *Supernatural* the night before.

The doctor's feedback had been vague and left us with no workable resolution. Gram's iron levels were low. Unsure why. Her blood pressure kept dropping unexpectedly. No explanation given.

We'd left the doctor's office with extra follow-up appointments planned and a directive for Gram to rest as much as possible.

There was no way Gram would put her feet up for longer than a couple of hours. She'd always struggled with downtime, which I understood because I was the same way. Too much to do, not enough time.

I'll sleep when I'm dead.

A chill crept along my spine at the thought, and I turned my attention back to the road as the stadium came into view, lit up by the setting sun, which accentuated the orange-and-black color scheme in vivid detail.

The floodlights over the field were already lit up, giant panels of white light that chased away shadows from every corner of the diamond.

Gram had decided to take an early dinner and head to bed before I left, and I'd made her promise to call me if anything felt wrong with her.

She'd told me to stop fussing and pushed me out the door.

I patted my pocket and relaxed at the boxy feel of my phone. She could call me if she needed. Coach Morales would just have to deal with me being on call during training.

The clubhouse was quiet, and my footsteps echoed off the walls in a way I wasn't used to. The team generated so much sound when they were in residence that any white noise seemed to be absorbed into the general din. It hadn't occurred to me how comforting those noises were until they were gone. Instead, my company was the smiling faces of players from the past, suspended in time. Some in the middle of performing great feats of sportsmanship, some holding up trophies and medals, while others were professional headshots with player numbers listed above their lifetime achievements for the Coyotes.

As a kid, I'd dreamed of having my face up on these walls, but as I wandered farther into the clubhouse toward the locker rooms, they felt like little more than lonely nostalgia. The game was done for every one of these men. They'd put down their bats and their gloves for a final time and stepped out of the spotlight to fade into obscurity.

"You're looking particularly maudlin. Are you ready to train?"

I jumped at the sound of her voice and spun to find she'd somehow snuck right up to my side like a ninja.

"Where did you come from?" I asked.

She shrugged and waved over her shoulder. "Back there. Are you ready? Or are you going to waste more of my time staring at the greats of years gone by?"

"Yeah, I'm ready. Give me a second, and I'll meet you on the field."

Without a word, she turned on her heel and left. Something in the set of her shoulders told me tonight was not the night to push her. I wondered what had happened between this afternoon and now to piss her off, then quickly reminded myself it wasn't my job to care.

The desire to poke the bear reared its head, but with a conscious effort, I forced myself to complete the trip to the locker rooms to retrieve my equipment and headed out to the field.

"You're twisting too much through the torso," she griped as I delivered a really fucking nice curveball. "It was wide."

"It wasn't wide."

"It was wide."

The woman was blind. Was it a hit to my ego, given recent events? Yeah, a little. It meant she couldn't properly appreciate my incredible good looks and how lucky she was to have received an orgasm from me, but it was the only explanation as to why she kept hounding me about my perfect drill.

"Go again and focus on stability through your core."

I humored her on the next pitch and watched the ball sail perfectly through the strike zone over the plate like it was responding to a formal invitation.

Not that I'd let her know that.

Her smirk told me she already knew.

"Okay, hit the showers. We're starting early tomorrow, so make sure you get some rest."

She'd been perfectly professional throughout the entire session. No snark, no subtle glances, none of her usual vibrancy. Even when I'd tried to needle her, she'd brushed me off with another drill and a complete lack of reaction. Something was eating at her, and I wanted to know what it was.

I rushed through a shower and threw on a soft T-shirt

and a fresh pair of sweats, hoping she didn't leave before I got out. As I shuffled into the locker room, I found her sitting at the small table, frowning at her laptop.

"Have you eaten?" I asked as casually as I could while stuffing my dirty clothes into a laundry bag.

"Ah, no. Not yet," she muttered, still consumed by whatever was on her screen.

"If we have an early morning tomorrow, you should probably fuel up. Today was a long day."

She grunted, arching one eyebrow.

I wandered up behind her to see she was watching old game tape.

It was the women's league. A few years old, by the quality of the footage and the fact the catcher was using finger signs to communicate with the pitcher. On the screen, the pitcher wound up and threw a curveball, the delivery slightly wide.

"Over rotation through the torso. Sometimes it'll still land, but it puts unnecessary strain on the body," she muttered without looking up.

The pitcher on the screen rubbed her shoulder, working the joint back and forth before the catcher tossed the ball back for the next pitch.

"Is that...?"

The footage cut to a closeup of the pitcher, and a younger version of the woman in front of me stared down the batter at the plate.

She snapped the laptop closed and turned in her seat.

"You're right. It's late. Time for dinner and bed."

The word bed sent heat rushing to my groin, but I reminded myself that just saying the word wasn't an invitation.

"Let me take you out to dinner."

I hadn't consciously planned to make the offer, but it made sense, I told myself. We had to eat, and we may as well do it together as colleagues who are both hungry. I offered her that piece of logic, but she didn't seem completely convinced.

I sighed. "Look. In all honesty, I had a rough afternoon, and I could do with a meal and maybe a beer to unwind. You kinda seem like you might be in a similar place. There's no angle here. I'm just asking if you want to grab a beer and a bite to eat after training, Coach."

"Why are you being nice?" she asked, collecting her belongings and turning toward the door.

"Let's call it a ceasefire. I'll be back to my usual pain in the ass self by tomorrow's practice."

I held the door open for her, waiting until she was clear before closing up behind us.

"Can't wait," she muttered.

"...so she pitched the book at the kid's head. Do you have any idea how hard it was not to high-five her?" Her eyes were alight as she told me the story of Zara's school suspension, buffalo wing held high in demonstration.

I chuckled along with her, having no trouble imagining her niece in that kind of trouble. She may not have been her mother, but there were certainly a lot of familial similarities between the girl I'd thrown balls for the other day and the woman in front of me.

"How did you end up helping to parent your niece? I honestly thought she was your daughter when I first saw her."

She nodded, taking a large bite of her wing and chewing thoughtfully. "I know. I heard you talking to her the other day. I've been told we look a lot alike, but I guess when her father is my twin, there's bound to be some similarity in his daughter. There's not a whole lot to tell. Zara's mother didn't want the job, so she left my brother with a newborn baby in his first year in the pros. I chose to put my career on hold and come home to help out. It hasn't always been easy, but I don't regret it."

The explanation made sense, but her delivery felt practiced. Too neat.

"So you prioritized your brother's career over your own? I have to say; that doesn't really sound like the Cami Morales I've come to know."

"You don't know anything about me," she snapped, then covered the outburst with a long pull on her beer.

"I know you're driven. That you know more than I'd like to admit about pitching mechanics and performance enhancement. It surprises me that you would have taken a step back just when your career was starting. That's all."

She grunted and pulled out her phone. "I'm going to need you to repeat that into the microphone. I'm going to play it back to you every time you challenge me on the mound."

"Not a chance in hell." I chuckled, and she relaxed back into her seat.

"Can we agree that we won't use this ceasefire to figure each other out? Can we just be here and ignore everything going on outside this bar?" she asked after a moment.

I reached across the table and offered her my pinkie finger. When she stared blankly at me, I gave it a wiggle. "You've never done a pinkie swear before?"

The smile I was looking for made the briefest of

appearances at the corner of her mouth, and she leaned forward and linked her finger through mine.

"To surface-level friendships and forgetting our problems," she declared, sitting back and retrieving her drink.

I'd drink to that.

The Irish pub we'd chosen was a popular spot for football fans, but it seemed that in this crowd I was as anonymous as the next person. I liked being able to eat my wings in peace across from my coach, who turned out to be surprisingly good company when she wasn't yelling at me.

"So when do they play their next game?" I asked.

Cami smiled softly, eyes focused on the near distance like she could see all her young players.

"This weekend. Saturday morning game before we meet for warmups. Zara is going to be opening pitcher this week, and she's been driving Christian crazy. She broke a window yesterday practicing her fastball in the yard."

I wanted to go to the game, but I didn't know if she would be open to it. Maybe I could just pass by during Nana's walk, and we could watch over the fence.

Would it be creepy for a full-grown man to watch an under-twelve's girl's baseball game?

Ugh. Probably.

But maybe I could convince her to invite me, and I could watch in a legitimate capacity. I hadn't been lying when I complimented Zara's skills. She'd clearly learned from the best.

Cami's eyebrows were raised, and I realized I'd missed a question while stuck in my own head.

"Sorry, what?"

"I said it's getting late. We should really get going. Early start tomorrow."

The clock above the bar read eleven p.m., and I knew she was right, but at the same time I didn't want the night to end. We'd managed to spend a significant number of hours alone together without trying to rip each other apart, and I didn't want to wake up tomorrow and act like it hadn't happened.

"Can I walk you to your car?" I asked, instead of saying any of the other stuff out loud.

At the end of the day, she was still my coach, and boundaries had to be maintained.

"Sure."

I let out a breath and slid to the edge of the booth while she did the same. As much as I didn't want this to end, a bigger part of me had worried I'd have to say goodbye and let her tiny self walk through the night alone to her car.

"Do you have far to get home?" she asked as we strolled through the mild night.

Above us, the stars were barely visible thanks to the light pollution from the city, but nothing could dull the full moon. I'd always been interested in the moon as a kid, but as I got older, I forgot to look up. For a long time, life felt too big. Too much. Every decision felt like the end of the world. Until a night not too long ago when I'd been outside with Gram, and she'd stopped short in the garden and craned her neck.

"If you ever need reminding of how small we are in the grand scheme of the universe, just look up. The universe is so vast, and we're so small. Just a blink in the timeline. We're only a small cog in a giant wheel, so we influence what we can and take comfort in knowing that all of this will be around a long time after we're forgotten. Just breathe, boy. Decisions will only affect your here and now. The world will go on spinning."

In retrospect, it could have been her kind way of telling me to get over myself, but it had also done its job. I wasn't the center of the universe, and there was comfort in that.

"Ah, yeah. It's a bit of a drive. The traffic is light at this time of night, though."

She nodded and came to a stop at a sleek-looking Volvo, and I realized it was time to say goodnight.

"Well...I guess I'll see you in the morning," I said, reluctant to leave.

"Yep, bright and early." A light breeze picked up and the scent of amber and lily filled my nose.

The ceasefire was still in place, and we'd both had a beer, just enough to relax. These are the excuses I gave myself later. But the truth was at that moment, I was powerless to resist stepping in toward her. Her breath caught in her throat as I backed her up against her door and paused with my mouth hovering just above hers.

"Tell me no," I whispered against her lips, both praying she'd have the sense to stop us, while dreading the idea of missing out on one more kiss.

"No." She fisted my T-shirt and pulled me the rest of the way down, licking into my mouth with a hunger that echoed my own.

Heat roared through my body as her hands clawed at my clothing, little grunts puffing from her throat as she tried to bring us closer together.

"Fuck, I want you," I murmured against her cheek, running my lips down her throat to nip at her collarbone.

My dick ached inside my boxers, not understanding why we couldn't just lay her out on the sidewalk and claim her like he'd been begging to since the first moment we laid eyes on her.

It may have been the snowball that did it.

"I live around the corner," she panted, scraping her nails through my hair as I nuzzled her breasts through her shirt.

I pulled away, studying her face for any signs she might not mean what she said.

"Don't look at me like that. We're grown adults. I'll give you a lift to your car in the morning. I mean...if you want to come home with me."

Yes! Yes! Yes! My cock chanted as I tried to clear my head enough to make an informed decision.

When a solid shake didn't work, I decided the fallout could be Tomorrow Gage's problem.

"I do," I managed to spit out, worried to say too much and ruin whatever was happening here.

"Good. Get in."

I almost gave myself a concussion hitting my head on the door frame as I dove into her passenger seat.

Luckily—or maybe unluckily, time would tell on that one—she hadn't been exaggerating about how close she lived, and in minutes we were pulling into the drive of a neat little single-story house. No time for second guessing.

As soon as we were through the front door, an invisible bell called an end to timeout, and I swept her into my arms.

"Bedroom?" I muttered as I ran my tongue up her throat, enjoying the salty taste of her skin.

"End of the hall on the right," she moaned, pulling my hair until sharp zips of pain ripped across my scalp.

In the back of my mind, a part of me would have liked to see where she lived. To know what knickknacks filled her private space and why each one was special enough to warrant a place here.

The larger part of me only cared about seeing more of

her skin and exploring all the ways I could make her come between now and sunrise.

The larger part was my dick. Just in case that wasn't clear.

Halfway down the hall, things almost took a turn for the worst when I tripped over an equipment bag left out in the middle of the floor.

"Oops," she chuckled, the sound turning into a moan as I bit her neck in punishment.

"If you leave a hickey, I'll kick your ass."

I hummed against her skin, tempted to leave one just to spite her, but we were playing a dangerous game, and as much as I liked to see her fire, I wouldn't put her career at risk.

"I'll leave one where no one will see it," I promised, balancing her on one forearm while I opened the door into her room, offering up a quick prayer of thanks at the sight of her king-sized bed.

I tossed her into the center of the mattress, letting her bounce as I reached behind my head and pulled off my T-shirt.

"Asshole," she said, the word petering off as she caught sight of my naked chest.

Hell yes, this was the reaction I wanted from the woman I was about to sleep with.

"You're looking a little overdressed there, Coach." I smirked at her as I toed off my sneakers and slid my sweats down my thighs.

"Uh huh," she muttered, eyes sweeping the length of me and pausing at my now-tight black boxers.

"Should probably do something about that."

Her little pink tongue darted out to swipe at her lower

lip, and a growl rumbled out of my chest before I could stop it.

Before I joined her on the bed, I slipped a condom out of my wallet, thanking an earlier iteration of myself for being prepared despite the dry spell I'd been in for the last too-many months.

As I knee-crawled over to her, she caught my eye and held it while she hooked her thumbs into the waistband of her sweats and pushed them to her ankles, revealing a cute but practical pair of black panties. Kicking them away, she pulled her top over her head next, and I had to squeeze my dick and remind him to settle down at the sight of her plain white T-shirt bra. Why was something so unassuming pushing me to the point of obsession?

Maybe because there was nothing performative about the way she moved. She knew what she wanted, and she was going to take it.

Simple as that.

"You are so beautiful," I breathed, meaning it with my entire soul.

"Shut up and get over here," she said, unhooking her bra in a practiced motion and throwing it off the edge of the bed.

When she reached for her panties, I knocked her hand away and took over the job, slowly sliding the fabric over her knees and down to her ankles before tracing the path back up with my lips. Over her calves to the inside of her knees where I drew circles with my tongue until she relaxed and let me push my way higher to her inner thigh. I left the hickey I promised and caught a smack on the back of my head, then I finally got to where I desperately wanted to be.

Her pussy was stunning. Pink and plump and desperate for a little attention. Settling onto my stomach, I blew a gentle puff of air over her in greeting and was rewarded with a full-body shiver. Running my nose over her soft skin, I could still smell that intoxicating mix of amber and lily. I wondered if it was her soap, or maybe just the way she smelled. Either way, I couldn't get enough.

"Do you have a plan here? Or do you need directions in bed, too?" she asked, the slightest strain in her voice betraying her need.

I huffed a laugh and finally took my first taste.

Fucking. Perfect.

I worked my tongue over her in broad strokes, taking note of the small whimpers and twitches of her hips. Learning her. Discovering what brought her closer to the edge, and what kept her hanging in a suspended state of pleasure until her fist tightened in my hair.

"Stop fucking around and make me come."

"Yes, ma'am."

Her thighs tightened around my ears with the next lick, and in seconds, she was screaming my name as she thrust her pussy against my lips, drawing out the bliss of the moment. As her body relaxed into the sheets, I lapped at her again, enjoying the way her body shuddered and ready to get her there again. With a firm hand, she pushed my head away and closed her knees.

"Too sensitive," she muttered, holding out a hand in invitation.

Spoil sport.

Respecting her boundary, I shuffled up the bed and stretched out beside her.

Her face was flushed the most perfect pink, her hair a riotous halo around her head. She'd never looked more beautiful, and I wondered how the hell I'd managed to get here.

"Do you have a condom?" she asked.

I held up the foil packet I'd palmed earlier.

"Do you plan on wearing it sometime before we have to go to work?"

I wasn't sure how she could turn me on so much while also making me feel like an incompetent idiot, but my dick was completely on board with her plan. I ditched my boxers and smirked at her soft gasp, then rolled the condom over my length and waited for further instruction.

"Come here." She let her knees drop out to the sides, and I rolled over her, positioning myself at her entrance before I paused.

"I want to kiss you, but I should brush my teeth first."

Peyton had hated me kissing her after I ate her out. Actually, she hadn't been too keen on me doing that either. She'd been more of a military sex on your birthday and maybe if I won the title kind of lover.

For me...anyway.

I swiped a hand over my mouth and eyed the door across the room, wondering if it was an ensuite and if there could possibly be an available spare toothbrush.

"Idiot," Cami said, breaking into my thoughts as she palmed the back of my head and brought my mouth to hers. As she took control of my mouth, she wrapped her legs around my hips, and then I was sliding into the warmest, most inviting place I'd ever been.

I wanted to live here.

Yes, that was my dick talking, and I wasn't inclined to disagree. Cami groaned as I bottomed out inside her, her body tightening around me as I breathed through the warning zaps of pleasure in my lower back.

Don't fuck this up and go too early.

When I trusted myself not to blow as soon as I started

moving, I pulled halfway out and slid all the way back in, setting a gentle rhythm that felt too much and not enough all at once.

"More," she groaned, digging her nails into my ass, and it finally started to sink in that I wasn't with the same woman I'd been with for the last eight years. Cami was different.

Someone who would tell me exactly what she wanted, and make it happen if I didn't get the fucking memo.

Right on cue, she pushed at my shoulder, flipping our positions so she could ride me. Our pace quickened, and I groaned as the new position pushed me deeper.

"Ohh...fuck. Yes."

Her breasts bounced as she increased the pace, her hips grinding over me in a way that I knew I wasn't going to be able to sustain for long. Her dark hair hung down her back in a tangled mess as she arched, chasing the sensations building inside her. To help her along and distract from my own impending orgasm, I found her clit with my thumb, rubbing fast circles that made her movements stutter. A long whine fell from her lips.

"Come on me, baby. I want you to squeeze my cock so tight."

With a short scream, she came, trembling on top of me as I gave in to my own release. It was sweaty, messy, and so damn perfect. After a long moment where we both caught our breath, she rolled off to the side, and I immediately missed her weight on top of me.

"We should definitely get some sleep," she said, sliding beneath the covers.

I slipped off the bed and took care of the condom, thankful the door did lead to a bathroom with a wastebasket. When I returned to the room, I pulled my boxers back on before joining her beneath the sheets.

Like I'd been doing it for years, I pulled her body into mine and settled down for sleep with the scent of amber and lily in my nose.

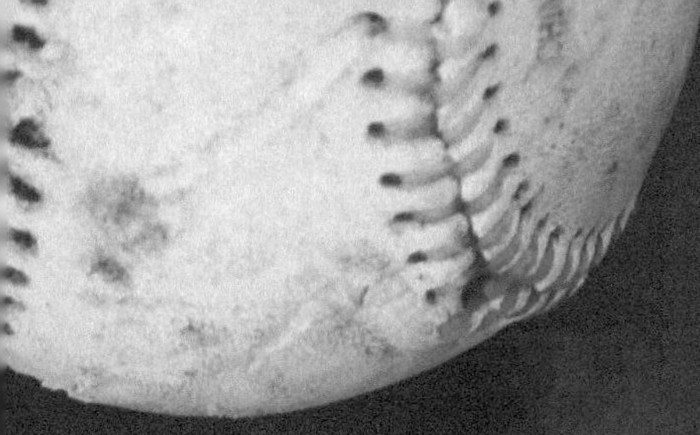

CHAPTER TWELVE

Cami

My alarm sounded far too early the next morning, and for a moment I couldn't understand why rolling over to turn the thing off was so difficult.

"Why is there noise?" a deep voice rasped into my hair.

The arm around my waist tightened, and moving became even more difficult as the unwise decision I'd made the night before threatened to make me late for work.

"We have to move. Early training, remember?"

His responding grunt did nothing to convince me he intended to move any time before midday.

"Gage. We have to go."

"I have a better idea," he murmured, hot breath ghosting across my ear. A shiver worked down my spine as he burrowed under the covers and turned me onto my back.

"Gage—"

His warm, wet tongue ran over my center. Damn, why did he have to be so good at that?

In his defense, he had me screaming in no time, and the day seemed a little brighter walking out the door riding a post-orgasm glow.

I'd had a quick shower before we left, but Gage had refused, claiming he'd grab one at the clubhouse so he could change into clean clothes at the same time.

I dropped him at his car and reminded him to go straight to the stadium and shower before training started. He paused with one leg poised in the footwell of his car.

"Maybe I won't have one at all. I love smelling you in my beard. It'll make it easier to ignore you when I'm on the mound."

He was still an asshole.

Training went by in a blur of ball-handling and pitching drills, with the odd set of sprints when the players started to slack off. I was beginning to realize that the job I'd signed up for was often comparable to babysitting just for two dozen odd overgrown boys. They were competitive, easily distracted, and still prone to laughing at fart jokes, much to the chagrin of the poor physiotherapist who happened to be working on Bailey at the time of the incident.

All of that would have been manageable if it weren't for the pranks. Chuck Bates considered himself the lead in prank engineering and had been responsible for both the sour milk smell in the now-vacant locker nearest the showers in the locker room, as well as the flooding of the visitor's bathrooms at the end of last season.

I'd been informed that I wasn't truly part of the team until I'd been subjected to one of Chuck's pranks, but so far, I'd managed to avoid it with a neat mix of intimidation and threats of suicide runs. Doug, the equipment manager, had not been quite so lucky and had spent the day sorting through tens of boxes of assorted bats. Some were plastic, some foam, and some the high-quality maple wood bats the men needed for game day.

I stayed back after practice to help Doug sort through the boxes, helping him devise plans for revenge that ranged from itching powder in his game-day pants, to replacing his bat with one of the ones we'd spent two hours sorting through. In the end, Doug decided not to poke the bear and had headed home, claiming that he'd be dreaming of bats for the next week.

As I strolled out of the player's entrance, I noticed a heavily pregnant woman loitering nearby.

"Can I help you?" I asked, holding my hands up in surrender as she let out a squeak and whipped around. The last thing I wanted was to scare her into early labor.

"I...I'm looking for Gage Wilson. Is he around?" She rubbed her belly, and as my eyes followed the movement, a sinking dread settled in my gut.

"No, I don't think he is," I said, unable to look away from her stroking hand.

She was a small woman, not much taller than me, with long dark hair and navy-blue eyes. Those eyes narrowed on me in a way that told me she was used to getting what she wanted.

As quickly as the sense of impending conflict rose, it dissipated as she let out a soft laugh. "Oh, this isn't his. Don't worry about that. I'm not here to cause a scandal. I'm just an old friend looking to reconnect. He doesn't seem to be answering his phone, and his gram said he spent most of his time here, so I figured..." She shrugged, indicating the stadium.

I returned her smile, still unsure as to why she'd chosen to turn up at the stadium afterhours to speak to a man who wasn't responsible for her current state. The same man who had woken me up with his tongue only twelve hours earlier.

"Well, maybe you'd have better luck on a game day," I said, already done with the conversation.

I wondered if the girls would be up for an impromptu taco night. We could drop Amber with Christian so Marina could have a margarita or two and just unwind while I debriefed them on everything I was doing to fuck my life up with Gage.

"What's your name?" the woman asked, tilting her head like a bird watching a worm.

"Cami. I'm one of the coaches here, and I need to get going."

"Nice to meet you, Cami. I'm Peyton." She didn't offer her hand, but she waited, like her name should mean something to me.

I didn't know her from a bar of soap and was about ready to tell her exactly that when she broke her creepy stare.

"I guess I'll see you around then, Cami."

She waddled off with a small wave that left me feeling complicit in some unknown wrongdoing.

I didn't like her.

Hopefully, her baby came sooner rather than later, and she left Gage the hell alone.

Not that he was any of my business. We'd had a couple of moments together, and they were done. It would be stupid to go any deeper, because despite what people kept telling me, I wasn't into self-sabotage.

But sometimes shit happened.

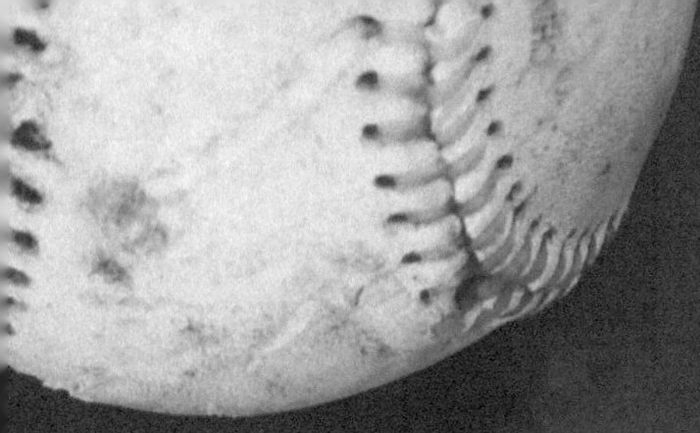

CHAPTER THIRTEEN

Gage

I SHOULDN'T BE HERE.

I'd had the thought playing in my mind on repeat for the last few blocks, but it hadn't made me turn around. Nana panted happily on the end of her leash—something that was more for show than function, seeing as she always walked perfectly to heel. Nothing bothered her. Not dogs, or people, or that one squirrel who tried to start shit with her every fall.

She just didn't let anything get to her.

I wished I could be the same way.

But there was one person who was very much getting to me, and the fact she had barely looked at me since the night we spent together was making me do crazy things.

Like turning up at her niece's baseball game hours before I had to be on the mound for my own game.

Gram was resting after another sleepless night, and I'd told myself that Nana deserved to get out of the house while the weather was fine. We'd started just walking the block, but when she turned her head toward the park, my feet had kind of...followed.

And now here we were at the edge of the fence, with me trying to decide if I looked more or less like a stalker by staying on the outskirts.

On a bench to the side of the field that had been set up as a temporary dugout, wearing a bright pink jersey and her hair in her signature ponytail, Cami was in her element shouting directions and encouragement for her batters and cheering as one of her players stole third.

It wasn't that she was an unenthusiastic coach when we were playing, but seeing her here, with the next generation of female talent, she really shone.

The crack of a bat pulled my attention back to the game, and I let out a whoop as a girl with dark hair and eerily similar features to her coach took off running. The fielders hadn't been ready for her, and she rounded second base before they were able to retrieve the ball.

"Go! Go!" I yelled as she tipped third and sprinted for home.

The ball sailed toward the catcher, the speed and accuracy far superior to what I would have expected from ten-year-olds, and I held my breath as Zara raced against the ball.

"Safe."

Half the crowd erupted as girls in pink jerseys spilled out of the dugout to jump on their teammate. Nana let out a howl of support as I punched the air, caught up in the excitement of the moment. Cami's head whipped in my direction, and for half a moment, I considered hiding behind my dog and hoping she didn't see me.

Nana was the same size as a miniature horse, so it

wasn't quite as bad of a plan as it sounded. Even at this distance, I could see her ponytail swinging as she shook her head, and just when I thought I should leave, she waved me over.

"Couldn't keep away?" she called as Nana and I picked our way along the fence line, ignoring the muttered speculation that followed me.

In football spaces, I could be a nobody, but anyone who knew baseball in this town knew exactly who I was, and that wasn't arrogance talking; it was just fact.

"I wouldn't have missed that for the world." I smiled.

"Gage! You came! Did you see my home run?" Zara bounced out of the dugout and ran up to the fence, sticking her fingers through the wire to say hello to Nana.

"I saw it. Great hit."

Zara positively glowed at the praise and brushed Cami off as she tried to pull her fingers away from Nana's seeking tongue.

"She won't bite. She's about as chill as an animal can possibly be."

Cami gave Nana a dubious look but stopped trying to physically remove Zara from the area.

"Will you stay for the rest of the game? And come for ice cream afterward? My friends didn't believe me when I told them we did batting practice together. Can we do it again?"

"I'm sure Gage can't stay too long. He has a game tonight, remember? That's why I have to drop you home after ice cream. We both need to get to the stadium for warmups."

The little girl deflated, and I immediately started mentally shuffling my day to make sure I could spend it with her.

"Don't let her fool you. Little girls are better con artists than politicians."

Zara glanced at her aunt, back to me, and dropped the puppy-dog expression in favor of a grin. "Maybe next time?"

"Yeah, next time," I agreed, not completely sure what next time would entail.

"Sucker," Cami said with a laugh, backing up toward the diamond. "Stay for the game if you want, but if you don't, I'll see you this afternoon."

I stayed for the whole game.

The St Louis Snipers were giving us a run for our money, and as the crowd belted out *Take me out to the ball game*, there was a solid chance the game was going to go into a tenth inning if they kept matching us run for run in the next two-and-a-half innings.

"Their pitcher is holding back on his fastballs," I said to Cami, eyeing Smith Warren as he stepped up to the plate. As our best hitter, we needed him to deliver a home run and boost the team's morale.

"He isn't holding back on purpose. He doesn't have the power because he has a tear in his shoulder. See the way he's relying on his rotation to deliver the power? He's going to tire quickly. Probably why he didn't start."

I could see exactly what she meant as he released the ball, and this time, Smith connected with the ball with a satisfying crack. Players in St Louis's black-and-green scrambled in the outfield to get under the ball, but it was one of those moments that reminded me that Smith was a force to be reckoned with as the ball kept flying on and on, and straight into the crowd. As one, every person in the dugout jumped to their feet. The noise was deafening as Smith headed off the field, head lowered with a quiet smile on his face.

"That's what I like to see," Coach Byers announced.

The home run was the push the Coyotes needed to take back the game, and by the time we got to the bottom of the ninth, they had no hope of catching us. Especially as I struck out their second hitter.

As the next batter stepped up to the plate, Bailey got into position. "Curveball," my hat chirped.

I shook my head.

"Slider," came next.

I nodded and made the pitch.

"Ball," called the umpire.

Fuck.

"Curveball," my hat chirped again.

Damn it, fine. I nodded and pitched, swallowing a curse as the bat connected and the player took off running for first base. The noise of the crowd dropped before doubling in volume, and the dugout cleared out as every member of our team sprinted onto the field to tackle Daxon Fields, the rookie, who had just caught out St Louis's last player of the game.

Bailey stood from behind the plate, laughing as he pulled his helmet off. "Damn, rookie," he shouted as the team escorted Fields to the clubhouse.

At the edge of the crowd, I caught a glimpse of Cami, her face flushed with excitement, eyes bright as she tried to herd men twice her size off the field.

She belonged here.

The thought sent both pride and guilt rushing through me.

I had spent the last few months learning Cami Morales; at first, to prove to myself she wasn't like the last woman I'd cared for, and more recently because she was a fascinating enigma of a woman who I needed to figure out. There was more to the story of why she left the women's league, and while I suspected it had something to do with her shoulder injury, I wanted her to open up to me. To tell me the story on her own.

She was a brilliant tactician who knew her shit when it came to baseball, and while it had worked out in our favor that she was available to coach us, it seemed criminal that she wasn't stopped in the street by people wanting to talk baseball like I was. Like I'm sure her brother was when it came to football.

The other side of all of this was that I knew what we'd been doing, coming together in these increasingly desperate clashes, could destroy everything she'd worked to rebuild. She was a new coach fucking around with an established player in the league. If it came out, her career would end in a heartbeat, while I'd get off with an admonishment at most.

It wasn't fair.

If I were a better man, I'd leave her alone. Give her space and keep everything purely professional. But as we left the field, I couldn't stop watching her ponytail swing against her back and remember how her hair flowed over her naked breasts while she rode me. The small noises she made as she chased her pleasure haunted me, disturbing my dreams in the best possible way. And her scent...

I'd stopped by a department store on the way home from practice the other night and tried to find that amber-and-lily combination in a perfume. Nothing had smelled quite right.

Which was probably a good thing because purchasing a fragrance based on the smell of my coach was probably a level of obsession I shouldn't entertain.

It didn't stop me regretting the missed chance to look for it when I'd spent the night in her bedroom.

Consumed by these thoughts, I didn't hear my name called at first. I was much more interested in watching the flex of Cami's ass under her sweats.

It wasn't until she turned and pointed out the interloper that I registered the presence.

And immediately wished I hadn't.

Peyton hadn't changed.

I mean...she had in the way her pregnancy had advanced significantly since I last saw her, when she packed up her belongings and told me I wasn't what she needed at this point in her life, but the secrets behind her eyes, the meek posture, the entitlement to my attention, that was all the same.

I turned back toward the clubhouse, intent on continuing to ignore this unwanted blast from the past, but Cami caught my arm.

"She came here the other day. I think she needs to talk to you."

My chest tightened at the news Cami had kept something from me, though the logical part of my mind reminded me there was no way she could have known who Peyton was.

"No, she wants to talk to me. There's a difference," I grumbled.

She cocked her head, studying me in a way I enjoyed despite the situation. Especially since she hadn't let go of my arm.

After a moment, she nodded, stepping back. I missed

the contact immediately and barely caught myself before reaching for her hand. There were too many witnesses.

"Come with me?" I asked instead, trying for an even voice. I must have missed the mark, because her face softened, and she made the first move toward my ex-girlfriend.

"What are you doing here?" I asked as soon as we were close enough.

The crowd was thinning, most people following the team to the doors of the clubhouse, while the fans funneled out into the parking lot on the other side of the stadium, but I kept my voice low to avoid drawing attention anyway.

"I wanted to see you."

"Why?"

Beside me, I could feel Cami's gaze burning into the side of my head. She'd seen me mean. Hell, I'd made preseason training as difficult as I could. Back then, all I'd known was that she looked like Peyton, she had a child—or so I thought—and she wanted to change me.

I'd been wrong about all of it.

She'd never seen me cold.

Honestly, I'd never been cold. But as I looked between Cami and Peyton, I couldn't believe I'd ever get the two confused.

"Why is she here?" Peyton asked, lifting her chin toward Cami.

"She's my coach. She can be wherever the hell she wants to be. Now, why are you here?"

"You didn't answer my calls."

"And that didn't tell you something?"

Her eyes filled with tears, and I took a half-step back.

"Gage. What happened to us?"

I opened my mouth. Closed it. Wondered what the actual fuck she was thinking.

In my mind's eye, I saw that final day.

The pregnancy test had been in the wastebasket in the bathroom, and I hadn't known what it was when I first found it. Two pink lines. I'd fished out the packaging and had to sit down as it hit home that something I'd never even considered was going to be part of my life.

A baby.

As soon as my legs had worked again, I'd found my phone and started searching jewelry stores. Things hadn't always been perfect with Peyton, but if we were having a child, it deserved to have a family. I was going to have to look at renovating the house. I'd been planning to offer the spare room to Gram because she was so alone in her big house, but if there were a baby on the way, we could all live here together.

In the space of an hour, I'd come up with a plan to reshape our whole lives for this new little being.

Peyton had come home from work tired and out of sorts, but I understood why and had a pregnancy-safe dinner waiting for her.

"We need to talk," she'd said.

"It's okay. I know," I'd replied, trying and failing to keep my smile at bay.

The tears were unexpected.

"It was a mistake."

"It's all right. We can deal with this together."

She shook her head and moved away from me.

"No. Moving in with you was a mistake."

Her face was blank. Tears still tracking down her cheeks as she took another step away from me.

"What...?"

"I'm pregnant, Gage."

"I know. I found the test—"

"It's not yours."

I knew the words she spoke were English, but some fundamental flaw in my processing kept them from making sense in my mind.

"Not...?"

"Not yours. Fuck, how could it be? When was the last time we had sex?"

I couldn't give her an answer. She was always tired from work or busy with one of her projects.

I was beginning to think 'project' could be code for another man.

"How long?"

"Since we had sex?" She huffed and looked away.

"How long have you been fucking someone else?"

"You seriously expect me to stay in this house alone while you travel all over the country for half the year?"

"It's my job!"

"Well, that's not my fault. I can't...I'm leaving. We're done."

Within an hour, she'd packed up our life and walked out without further explanation, leaving me with an empty home, a broken heart, and a pregnancy test that had nothing to do with me.

I blinked away the memory and stared down the woman I'd been willing to marry.

"You made a choice—several choices—about what you wanted your life to look like, and I wasn't a part of it."

Cami shifted, her arm brushing mine in a subtle show of support. I don't know if she'd put together that Peyton was an ex, but if not, the cat was out of the bag.

"He doesn't want anything to do with the baby." A sob burst from Peyton.

I glanced around quickly, worried about witnesses of the reporter variety.

"Why don't we all just duck in here," Cami suggested, guiding us toward a storage closet. Not ideal, but at least a little more private.

As we shuffled inside and arranged ourselves in the small space, Peyton sniffled, shuffling a little closer to me, even as I tried to keep the space between us. It became somewhat of a dance that ended when I physically lifted Cami into the space between us.

"Why is she here?" Peyton asked again, eyeing my hands where they conveniently hadn't yet released Cami's hips.

"As his coach, his well-being is my priority. He asked me to be here as a witness, and I'm obligated to fulfill that request," Cami responded, brushing my hands off.

"And how, exactly, are you prioritizing his well-being?"

"What's that supposed to mean?"

Peyton slid her eyes over Cami in an assessment that was far too calculating for my liking.

"Are you fucking my man?"

"What the fuck, Peyton?" Had she always been like this?

"It's a reasonable question. Yes or no. Coaches are meant to be professional, but this seems like you're taking advantage."

"Do not try me, bitch. Pregnant or not, I'll make you wish you'd never met him if you don't back the fuck off and get out of my stadium."

A big part of me perked up hearing Cami put Peyton in her place. Yup, it was my dick again, but I didn't have time for this now. Peyton was threatening to fuck with Cami's career, and I couldn't let that happen.

"You really haven't noticed how much you look like me,

have you? It seems a whole hell of a lot like when he couldn't have me, he found a cheap replacement. Gage, when you're ready to talk like an adult, you know where to find me."

With that parting jab, Peyton left the closet, taking all the air in the room with her.

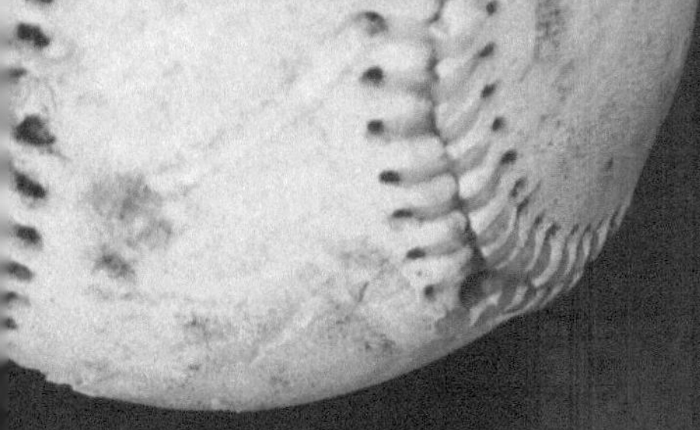

CHAPTER FOURTEEN

Cami

My name is Cami Morales, and I am an expert at self-sabotage.

As I sat in a booth alone at Mabel's Bakehouse waiting for my friends to show up, I had to reluctantly admit I owed my brother an apology.

Without conscious thought, I'd epically fucked up my career for a second time, and now I had to figure out what the hell I could do to fix it.

So I called in reinforcements.

Ridley arrived first, bouncing into the room wearing a Blizzards jersey and a huge smile.

"It feels like forever since we last caught up. Why do you have to be such a busy professional woman these days? I miss you." My vision was temporarily obscured by a riot of bubblegum pink curls as she leaned in for a hug.

"How are you doing?" she asked, sitting back and waving to Bomb to bring over the coffeepot.

"Destroying my life, thanks for asking. And you?"

Ridley gave me an admonishing look before thanking Bomb for her coffee.

"It can't be that bad. Hold on to the story for just a minute, though. Marina and Gia were just parking outside, so you can tell us all at once, and we'll fix it."

"You mean Marina will fix it."

"That's what I said." Ridley gave me a cheeky grin as the other two women in question entered the cafe with an unwelcome, hulking form in tow.

"Why did you bring my brother?" I complained as they slid into the booth around me, simultaneously making me feel loved and claustrophobic.

"Because I heard you guys were getting pastries without me. What's the big deal?"

"This is your disclaimer: if you stay here, you're going to hear about me having sex."

"Then I reserve the right to vomit."

"You can't vomit because then I'll vomit, and that's not fair to the staff here."

Christian sighed. "Fine. Pretending you aren't my sister for the next twenty minutes and...go."

He pretended to set a timer on his watch, and Marina slapped his hands down, shaking her head before turning her attention back to me.

"Now, what's the problem?"

"Gage Wilson triggers my fight-or-fuck response," I blurted.

Christian gagged.

I gagged.

Marina slapped the back of his head and refocused on me.

"Elaborate, please."

I told them the whole story from the start. The kiss. The late-night training session that ended in a sleepover. The visit from the ex.

"I think you were right," I said, barely able to look Christian in the eye. "I have been self-sabotaging. Just like last time. Why am I like this?"

I slumped in my seat, defeated. There was no coming back from this. All Peyton had to do was report misconduct to management at the Coyotes, and my career in professional baseball was done.

All because I kept allowing myself to be drawn in by someone I hated.

Did I actually still hate him?

I ignored the little voice in the back of my head in favor of self pity.

The table was quiet, and that, more than anything, led me to believe I was fucked.

"Have you spoken to Coach Byers about this?" Christian asked.

"Ah, yeah. Kind of? I did the first couple of times, but he seemed to think it was a self-sabotage thing too. I guess I was the only idiot who didn't see it."

Marina was too quiet.

The resident psychologist was the voice of reason in our motley crew, and I couldn't recall a time when she hadn't willingly weighed in on a problem. Either she was stumped, or she was working out how to tell me something I didn't want to hear.

Shit. I hoped it was the first one.

"Apple danish?" Bomb dropped the plate in front of me, and I forced a smile, despite the fact my stomach turned at the sight of food.

"Is there any chance," Marina started, her Australian

drawl more pronounced as she eased into the suggestion, "That the reason you didn't see it as sabotage is because you genuinely like him?"

"No." The word was out of my mouth before I had time to even consider the question.

'Like' wasn't in my vocabulary when it came to Gage Wilson. I tolerated him. We were extremely sexually compatible. But *like*?

No. He pissed me off too much for that term.

"Zara said he turned up at her game on Saturday," Christian said, taking my distress as an opportunity to steal my apple danish.

I glared at him as he devoured half the pastry in a single bite.

"He did. I guess he lives near the field and came across the game while walking his horse."

"He has a horse?" Gia asked.

"Ah, no. But it's too big to be classified as a dog, so what else would you call it?"

"A dog," Christian said through his mouthful of the rest of my danish. "Just because you're small doesn't mean other animals should be reclassified to fit your size expectations."

I flipped him off and turned back to the helpful people at the table.

"I think you need to decide what you want out of all of this, and what is realistically possible at this point." Marina said, proving psychologists weren't always as helpful as they thought they were.

"I want to be the pitching coach for the Chicago Coyotes," I said firmly, like I hadn't been saying it all along.

"So choosing your way ahead will have to align with that goal in mind. What is the first thing you need to do?"

Christian raised his hand. “I could go set this guy straight. I already think he needs a visit just for putting the image of Cami having sex in my head.”

He gagged.

I gagged, then kicked him under the table.

Marina sighed. “How about we call that Plan B, okay?”

Christian stole my coffee cup and sat back, satisfied with his contribution.

“Stop stealing my stuff,” I grumbled, but made no attempt to retrieve the cup. My stomach was roiling too much to ingest anything anyway.

“I guess I get ahead of things. Go and speak with Coach Byers; let him know about Peyton and what’s happened between me and Gage. Then put barriers in place to being alone with Gage and commit to keeping the relationship professional. I can’t change what I’ve done, but I can move forward in the way that best supports my goals.” I glanced at Marina and felt the breath ease in my lungs when she nodded.

“I think it’s all a bit romantic, really,” Ridley said. “I mean, an illicit affair between work colleagues, a really hot athlete—don’t look at me like that, Christian, you know he’s hot—amazing orgasms...it’s like something out of a romance novel. The only thing missing is the hockey.”

“The hockey?” I asked, glancing at her jersey.

“Uh, yeah. Hockey romances are the best. Although I suppose baseball is kinda hot too. Something about those tight pants.”

“She’s right,” Gia decided, nodding in Ridley’s direction. “It sounds like something out of a *Shifting Sands* episode.”

Shifting Sands was the long-running soap opera Gia had been cast in the previous year. The plots were outlandish and the romance over the top, so I didn't entirely appreciate the comparison.

"Thanks, guys."

Marina was right, though. I needed to get my head in the game and remind myself that I had every right to be sitting at the coach's table, so I had to start acting in my own best interest, and the first step was ignoring Gage Wilson.

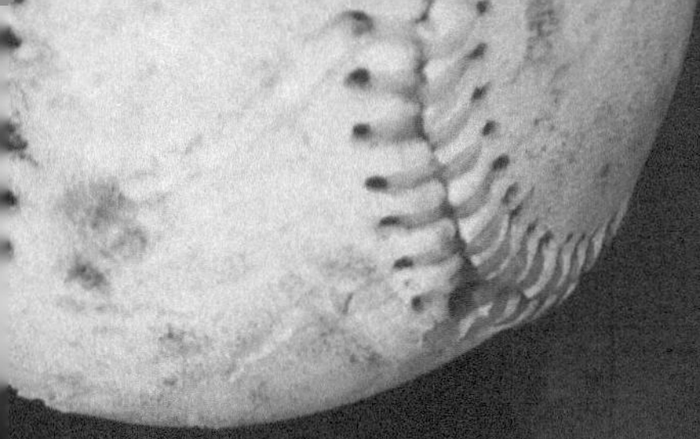

CHAPTER
FIFTEEN

Gage

Fucking Peyton.

A week later, I was still walking on eggshells, waiting for my life to explode around me as her threats lay heavy over the stadium like a fine coat of oil, dripping down the walls and threatening to make everything slide right off the earth.

Cami had been avoiding me for the last few days, allowing assistant coaches to step in for one-on-one training, and slipping out the door any time I sought her out.

I'd even gone so far as to text her, under the guise of checking in about training, but she'd responded with a single text confirming the details and adding: *It's time to focus on our job*. I'd asked her to elaborate but hadn't heard back.

The thought of going to her house had crossed my mind, but even I could tell that would be crossing the line.

So all I could do was respect her boundary and keep my distance.

All of this meant that when I walked through my front door on Tuesday night, exhausted from extra self-imposed training sessions combined with over a week of insomnia, I wasn't in my finest mood. Stomping through the front door, I gave Nana an absent pet on the head on the way to my bedroom and ignored her soft whine in favor of stripping off and climbing into the shower. The water pounded over my head, the warm rivulets running down my back causing a contrasting warm/cool sensation that did nothing to pull me out of my mood.

I'd worked my ass off to move on after she abandoned me.

Never mind that it was the theme of my fucking life.

My parents left.

Peyton left.

Now Cami was leaving me and, for some reason, that one ached more than the others. Maybe because it was fresher. Maybe because she hadn't actually gone anywhere. She was still there every day, giving directions and striving to make us the team that takes home the Diamond League title this year, but on the rare occasion she had to look at me, she looked through me.

Like I was nothing.

"It was just a stupid crush," I growled into the water. I barely knew her. I'd spent most of the time since I met her antagonizing her, and she'd gone toe to toe with me.

"Fuck."

Even now, the thought of her was making me hard. Instead of sinking to a new low, I cranked off the hot water and let the icy cold run over me.

The shot of cold was like needles over my skin,

numbing me out in a way I wished could penetrate right to my core.

Stop letting people in; that's how you get hurt.

Peyton had tried just once more, the night before, to reach out, but I rejected the call and finally blocked her number. That chapter of my life was done.

Shivers coursed over my body as I stood beneath the icy flow of water and tried to convince myself I had everything I needed. My career. My dog. Gram. What more could I ask for?

Instead of sulking in the shower like a prepubescent boy, what I needed to do was check in on Gram, see if she needed anything, and maybe suggest we do some knitting together. The clicking of the needles was soothing; the repetitive motion was a kind of meditation that always grounded me when things felt overwhelming.

Decision made, I shut off the shower and toweled off.

When I stepped out of the bathroom, pulling my T-shirt over my head, I almost tripped over Nana.

"Whoa, Nana girl. Careful, I didn't see you there."

She whined, paced toward the bedroom door, then back to me.

"What's wrong? Do you need to go out?" I led her through the house to the back door, but when I propped it open, I realized she'd gone a different direction.

"What's up?"

She sat outside Gram's door, going as far as to scratch at the wood when I didn't come closer.

"Is Gram taking a nap? Leave her alone; we'll wake her in a little while for dinner."

Nana whined again and let out a single bark.

My gut sank as Nana became more insistent by the second that we checked on Gram.

I'd barely turned the handle on the door when Nana used her weight to knock the door open, immediately going to the side of the bed where Gram lay on her side in darkness.

"Gram?" I whispered, reluctant to invade her space.

I hadn't stepped foot inside her room since I was a small boy, seeking comfort from nightmares. She would always roll over and pull back the covers, letting me slide into the divot of warmth where she'd been while she moved over to the cool side of the bed.

The air felt heavier now, an eerie kind of silence weighing down the dim room so that even Nana's soft panting felt muted.

"Gram," I said again, louder this time, as I took a hesitant step across the threshold. My heart pounded, my hands inexplicably shaking as I made my way one step at a time toward where she lay.

"Grammy?" I squeezed her shoulder, shocked again by how frail she felt beneath my fingers.

When had she become little more than skin and bone? My hand tightened of its own accord, but she didn't move. Didn't flinch. And something inside me broke.

The first sob took me out at the knees. I crashed to the floor beside her bed, barely able to see the light from the hall shining in her sightless eyes for the tears that filled my own.

Nana leaned her shoulder into my side as I gracelessly fell to pieces.

The one person in my life who had always sworn she would never leave me had been taken. Not because she wanted to go—no, I wouldn't believe she'd left me by choice—but because age was a bitch, and her beautiful mind was trapped in a body that couldn't keep up with her anymore.

I cried like the little boy I'd been when I first came to live with her. The one who didn't understand why Mommy and Daddy weren't coming to take me home. I cried until I couldn't hold myself up anymore, and then I curled up on the floor with Nana at my back and sobbed until dawn.

The next day was a blur, from the doctor's visit to the hospital room, where she was legally pronounced dead, to calls from the funeral home she'd arranged without my knowing.

Faceless people trying to pull my attention in various directions. Shoulder touches and soft words, and an aching loneliness that made it all feel like it was happening on the other side of frosted glass.

"Is there anyone you'd like us to call?" someone asked.

I shook my head. There was no one left.

Eventually, I found myself sitting alone in my quiet house, my dog by my side.

Memories of Gram's life flicked through my head in a sideshow of love and warmth, all of them now bearing the sepia cast of ancient history. Never to be seen again.

The thought of food drifted through my mind, there and then gone as my eyes finally focused on my phone and the several missed calls that I should have considered dealing with. Maybe tomorrow. For now, there was only one voice I needed to hear.

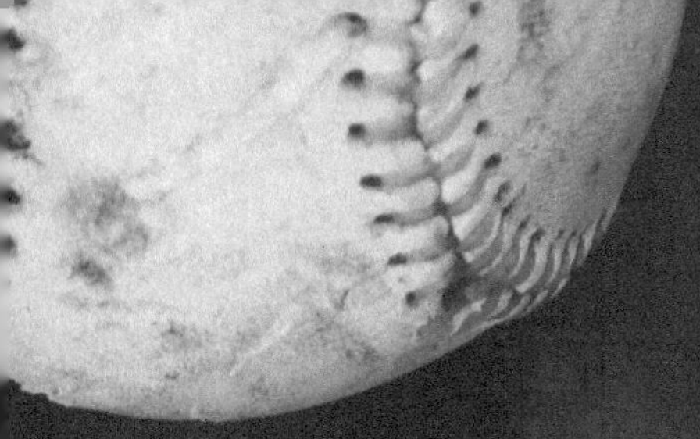

CHAPTER SIXTEEN

Cami

Gage wasn't at practice.

Despite my resolve to avoid contacting him, I didn't ask an assistant coach to follow up; instead, I started the players on an upper-body workout in the gym and slid out the side door. The call went straight to voicemail, and I tried one more time before leaving a polite message asking after his well-being and hanging up.

Maybe he'd spoken to Coach Byers. Winding through the halls, I tried not to let my imagination wander to things like trade deals and car wrecks. All the ways Gage could suddenly disappear from my life, then reminded myself once again that he wasn't in my life.

"Morales, I was about to come find you. Come in." The tone was measured, and missing some of the warmth that he usually greeted me with.

Shit.

What had happened?

No time to worry; I still needed to find out where Gage was.

"Hi Coach, I was wondering if Wilson had checked in with you today?"

He paused his typing and closed his laptop, waving me into his office. As I settled into one of the leather chairs opposite him, he leaned back and took a moment to study me.

"Management has received a formal complaint of misconduct between you and one of the players from a member of the public."

"A member of the public," I repeated, Peyton's face flashing in my mind.

Coach's face was an unreadable mask as he waited for me to process the news.

"What does this mean?" My mind was still struggling to change lanes from missing Gage to the threat to my career.

Coach leaned forward in his chair, resting his forearms on the desk as he continued to watch me. I wondered if he was a parent. He had major 'dad vibes'. I could picture his son or daughter cracking under the pressure of that stare and spilling all kinds of details without him saying a word.

After a long moment, he finally sat back and folded his arms.

"There are a few pieces of good news here. The person in question had no evidence of wrongdoing. Only speculation, which is not grounds for any administrative action beyond cursory investigations. The better news is that you have already informed me of the extent of the situation...right?"

"There was..."

"Did it happen on Coyote grounds?"

"No."

"Then I know everything I need to know at this point. The only thing I have left to ask you is...do you like fruitcake now?"

I huffed a laugh that came out almost like a sob as I came to fully appreciate the man across from me.

Definitely a dad, I decided as he waited for my answer.

I'd given him honesty, and in return, he was protecting me. Trusting me. The problem was that he'd asked me a question I didn't have an answer to.

"I...don't know. This job is my priority, and I would never do anything—anything else—to jeopardize it. I've taken a step back from...the fruitcake...because when it comes down to it, you were right. I was self-sabotaging. When I injured my shoulder, I scared myself. I lost my edge because my fear of failure on the mound was louder than my fear of not fulfilling my dreams. I used Zara's birth as an excuse to leave the league before someone found me out as a fraud, and I kept myself down for ten years. I don't want to be small anymore, and I really don't want to have my career threatened by a selfish ex-girlfriend who didn't know how to appreciate who she had. Maybe I've come to appreciate fruitcake, but it doesn't mean I'll let it be another reason I don't achieve my dreams."

I had no idea if any of that had made sense, but just acknowledging it—saying it out loud—felt like a weight was lifted from my shoulders, one I'd been carrying for over a decade.

"Good girl," Coach said. "You were a great pitcher, Morales, and you're shaping up to be an even better coach. I've been monitoring the players, and as far as I can tell, none of them are aware of anything between you and Wilson. You're keeping it professional, and as long as that continues until one, or both, of you leave the Coyotes, then

I don't see any reason why management needs to get involved. Just know, if any of that changes, I'm pleading ignorance, and you're on your own."

I chuckled as he gave me a friendly wink before growing serious again. "You said Wilson is missing?"

I checked my phone again but still hadn't had a return call.

"He's never late for practice, and he isn't answering his phone."

Coach nodded. "Okay, leave it with me. Go back to practice, and I'll call around and see if I can find him."

There was no part of me that wanted to leave while Gage could be lost, or hurt, or who knew what, but I'd just finished explaining that my job was my priority. So I had to prioritize it.

Practice was an exercise in patience; the entire team was off as Gage's absence echoed through the players. Everyone had tried to call him. All with the same result. Coach Byers announced that he hadn't been admitted to any of the local hospitals around midday, and while the news made it slightly easier to breathe, his continued absence affected every aspect of the player's performance for the afternoon. I ended up finishing the session with thirty minutes to spare.

"Hit the showers and come in tomorrow ready to work hard. We need you all ready for game day."

There was a general grumble of agreement as they all filtered off the field toward the clubhouse. At Coach Byers's office, I stopped in the doorway.

"Any word?"

He shook his head. "I'm thinking about stopping around at his house after work. See if he's home."

"I'll go," I offered.

He eyed me dubiously, then nodded.

"I need his address."

That made him smile. "You aren't there every night?"

I mock-gasped, pressing a hand to my chest as I quickly checked the hall for unwanted ears.

"That sounds like something someone who loved fruitcake would do. I'm still on the fence. It hasn't been...it's not like that."

"I'm teasing," he said, scribbling something on a Post-it note and holding it out for me. "Go make sure our boy is safe."

The sun was setting as I pulled up in front of a beautiful ranch-style home out in the suburbs. A green car sat around the side of the house, and in the drive was Gage's black SUV. As I unbuckled my belt, my phone buzzed in the cup holder.

"Gage," I answered, cradling the phone to my ear in my need to hear his voice.

"Cami?" His voice was little more than a croak.

"What's wrong? Where are you?"

The line went quiet.

Through the windshield, I watched the streetlights snap on as the sky began to fade into a wash of pink and orange.

A young woman in business attire strode past, attached to a tiny fluff ball of a dog by a thin leash.

"She's gone." The words were so soft I pulled the phone from my ear to check the connection.

"Who's gone?"

More silence. The house was dark, an empty void in the middle of a street of houses lit up where families would be just sitting down for dinner.

I pictured myself getting out of the car. Could feel the

gravel of his driveway beneath my shoes as I walked up to his front door. Was there a security light that would turn on to light my way up the steps? Or would I have to fumble my way in the darkness?

And when I got there, what next? A door knocker? A bell? Would I even be welcome inside? All these thoughts kept me rooted to my seat as the light faded piece by piece.

"My gram died last night."

I'd spent a lot of the last few months avoiding learning anything about Gage Wilson, but one thing that was clear to anyone who knew him was how much he loved his gram.

"I'm sorry."

"Don't be sorry. I can't...don't be nice to me right now."

"You want me to be...mean?"

"I want you to be real. You're the only real person I know, and now that I'm completely alone, that means so much more to me than you can possibly imagine. Tell me... something. Anything. Please."

I cast around for anything I could tell him. Something to distract him from the darkness he'd surrounded himself with.

"Okay, umm...have I ever told you I'm a sympathy vomiter?"

"No." His voice was laced with a curiosity that made me breathe a little easier after the hollowness of a few moments earlier.

"So one year Christian and I begged our parents to take us to the local fair. Now, I don't know if you've realized this about me, but I'm a little bit competitive."

He huffed a laugh.

"But that's nothing compared to how I am with my twin. I love him dearly, but I will fight to the death to avoid him ever getting one up on me. Anyway, he decided to lay down a challenge. For each ride we went on, we needed to eat a stick of cotton candy. So we eat the first stick and jump on the roller coaster. Then we eat the next one and go on the Octopus. We're both already a little green by this point, but neither of us is backing down.

"Anyway, we get to the third stick, and I decide to cheat, because Christian is twice my size and there's no chance I can hold as much cotton candy as he can, so when he calls for a bathroom break, I dissolve my entire stick of cotton candy in a water bucket while he's not looking. Anyway, the next ride is the tilt-a-whirl. It was always our favorite, though I have to say, I don't recommend it after that much sugar—even if you cheated and didn't eat it all.

"We make it through the ride all right, but as we step off, Christian holds his stomach. I go from feeling fine to having a heavy weight inside of me, and as soon as he starts tossing his guts, I'm right beside him doing the same. We thought it was a one-time thing, but then while I was in the pros we went out for a girl's night. I was the designated driver, and everything was fine until one of the girls asked me to pull over so she could be sick. Sure enough, next minute I'm out of the car bringing up the two sodas I'd drunk.

"Christian thinks it's hilarious, the bastard. But there you have it. Sympathy vomiter. I guess that's why I never looked into working in healthcare."

The sky was almost completely dark now, the navy-blue wash only broken by the lightest wisps of clouds.

"You don't talk about your parents."

I shrugged, even though he couldn't see me. "They like to travel. As soon as Christian and I were old enough to go to college, they left to see Europe and haven't been back since. They send a postcard every Christmas and a card for

Zara's birthday, and that's about it. I think Christian talks to them during football season."

"You're lucky you have your brother."

"Sometimes." I grinned. "He can be a pain in the ass, but I love him. He's my other half."

The sounds of fabric moving came down the line, and I wondered what he was doing. Was he in bed? Sitting on a sofa in the dark? I couldn't imagine the loss he'd just experienced, but I understood his absence a little better. Not everything had to be shared with others, but for whatever reason, he'd chosen to share it with me.

"Tell me another story?"

So I did. I told him about my first year in the women's league. About Christian getting drafted to the Engines and the way our life changed meeting Weston and Marina. I told him about Zara's kindergarten graduation, and the first time she hit a home run. I talked about everything and nothing, and before I knew it, the clock on my dash read one a.m., and my ass was asleep from sitting in one place for too long.

"Are you still awake over there?" I asked as the silence stretched over the line.

He hummed. "I was just wishing you were here. Thank you for answering your phone tonight. I know I was a shit to miss practice without letting anyone know."

"Umm..." I debated telling him where I was, but the decision was taken out of my hands when pain flared through my hip, and I knew it was time to get out and stretch. "I'm kind of outside."

A light flared over the front door, and Gage came striding out of the house in nothing but a loose pair of running shorts.

Even in the darkness, his face was ghostly, drained of its

usual color. Darkness ringed his bloodshot eyes, and he seemed somehow deflated.

"Why the hell didn't you come to the door, Morales? You've been sitting in this car trying to cheer up my morose ass for the last however many hours. Come inside."

I stood from the car, my spine cracking and popping as I straightened out of the slouch I'd adopted for far too long. The sadness lingered, but concern for my well-being had him hovering anxiously, looking for some way to care for me.

"Do you want something to drink? Coffee? Water? Herbal tea?"

"Actually, tea would be great. But I came here to check on you. How are you feeling? Can I do anything?"

He gave me a small smile as he filled a kettle with water and set it on the cooktop.

"She always insisted on making tea in a proper English kettle. She visited Europe when she was young and always told me stories about the soldiers at Buckingham Palace and eating pastries in Paris." He quieted as steam began to billow out of the jug.

"Gage?"

"You've already done more than enough." His eyes shone when he glanced back at me. "Thank you for being here."

"I was worried about you." Something hairy and wet brushed my knuckles, and I instinctively jumped back from his beast of a dog, but the animal just dropped to the floor, curling up and placing its giant chin on my toe.

"She was worried too, so I'll tell you both that I'm okay."

He filled two cups with boiling water and handed one across the counter. I accepted it with a smile and idly dunked the teabag as the silence settled around us again. Things felt different between us at that moment. Like all of the bullshit had been left at the door and we'd given ourselves permission to just be.

"Will you stay the night?" he asked after a while, his gaze fixed on his tea.

"Yes."

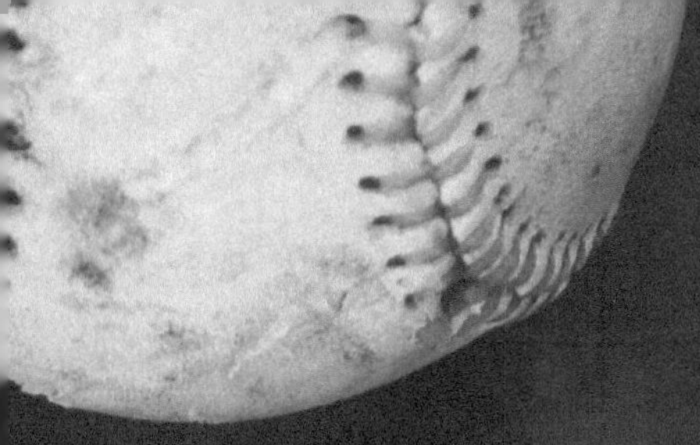

CHAPTER SEVENTEEN

Cami

The pillow beneath my cheek wasn't the silk one I was used to.

That was the first thought that crossed my mind as consciousness returned the next morning. I was warm, right on the edge of too warm. And I needed to pee.

A deep groan rumbled against the back of my neck as I wriggled out of Gage's tight grip and went in search of the restroom.

We'd passed out as soon as our heads hit the pillow in the early morning hours, Gage exhausted by the weight of his grief, while I had just never been a night owl. While his bedroom had been black as pitch, bright sunlight filtered in through windows in the hall, and I decided a detour to find my phone was needed.

Nana lifted her head with a small whine of greeting as I wandered into the kitchen, thumping her tail a couple of times before she closed her eyes to enjoy the patch of sunlight she'd curled up in.

Eight a.m. Shit. I dialed Coach Byers's number, immediately regretting not using the restroom first as nerves made my bladder problem worse.

When he answered, I explained the situation and how I'd stayed with him the night, barely resisting the urge to swear there hadn't been any 'funny business'. Coach asked if Gage would be good to play that afternoon, and I had to tell him that I honestly didn't know. I promised to have him call as soon as he woke up and ended the call with an agreement that I would be at the stadium within the hour.

Finding the restroom, I finally got some relief and slipped back to Gage's room.

He was beautiful, laid out against the sheets, and I felt the urge to do something for him surge through me. Crawling over the covers, I pressed a kiss to the underside of his jaw. He pulled in a long breath through his nose and relaxed, stroking a large palm through my hair.

"Relax and let me take care of you."

He mumbled sleepily and let his arms flop to the sides as I drew the bedding off his body. He may have still had his eyes closed, but as I reached the waistband of his shorts, it became apparent that at least one part of his body was wide awake.

I gripped his erection through the fabric, giving a couple of slow strokes to make sure he was conscious enough to consent, and when he groaned long and low, I took it as permission to continue.

Lifting the elastic over his bulge, I pressed a small kiss to the deep cherry tip before running my tongue along the underside.

"Cam," he murmured, resting his hand on top of my

head. Not gripping, not controlling, just there. An acknowledgement.

I sucked his length into my mouth, humming as I bobbed over him until his hips thrust up toward me of their own accord.

"Fuck," he muttered, his hands sliding down to grip the sheets. Even half asleep, he was still as polite as always.

I worked my fist over his length, loving how his eyes slitted to watch me work as his thighs grew more and more tense beneath me. Without breaking eye contact, I slid my lips back over his tip and sucked hard.

"Fuck. Coming," he muttered, stroking a hand over the side of my face in warning.

I kept up my pace, and a moment later, the bitter taste of his release pulsed across my tongue.

When he finished a few moments later, I straightened his shorts and rolled off the bed.

"Who were you talking to just before?" The words came out in a rumbling, satisfied slur that made me smile.

"Coach Byers. Everyone was worried about you yesterday."

He grunted, burying his face in his pillow.

"What are you doing?"

I paused with my sweats halfway up my legs. "I have to get into the stadium. We have a game tonight."

"Okay. Gimme a sec, and I'll come too."

"You don't have to..."

He heaved himself out of bed, his shorts so low on his hips that I could see his neatly trimmed pubic hair and the lines of the top of his deflating erection.

I averted my eyes but glanced back in time to see him pull the shorts up over his ass as he opened a hidden door in the wall. Damn. He had an ensuite.

I finished pulling on my clothes and shoes as behind the door a toilet flushed and water came on. A moment later he reappeared with wet hair and half an attempt at a smile.

"You ready?" he asked, pulling open another door to reveal a small closet. He slipped a shirt over his head and palmed a pair of sneakers before wandering out of the room. I followed him into the kitchen and watched him feed the dog before downing a glass of water over the sink.

"Should we drive in separately or together?"

There was only one right answer, especially given the conversation I'd had the day before, but I wanted to give Gage the freedom to choose whichever he needed that morning.

"What do you need?"

He crossed the room in two strides and took my face in his hands.

"Just this." He dropped his lips to mine in an achingly gentle kiss.

It wasn't like anything we'd shared before, our usual fire tempered in a moment that was at once sweet and terrifying.

I'd made a decision, and despite what Coach Byers seemed willing to compromise on, was it possible for us to keep this thing between us secret? I'd read those kinds of romance books when Ridley dragged me to book club, and they never ended well.

"I haven't brushed my teeth," I hedged, backing away from him.

"I don't care."

"I do."

He nodded and looked away, retrieving his phone from its charger. I was such a bitch.

"Gage—"

"Wow, I'm going to have to do something about all these missed calls. Hopefully, I'll be able to delete half of them just by showing up for practice today, huh?"

"Yeah."

"It's probably a good idea to take two cars; otherwise you'd have to go out of your way to either drop me home or pick up your car. It doesn't make sense, really."

"Peyton reported us to management."

Gage paused mid-rant and stared. "No, she didn't."

I nodded. "Coach didn't specifically say it was her, but someone reported us for misconduct, and no one else has seen us together."

He ran a hand through his hair and let out a rough curse. "I'm sorry. I didn't mean to bring any of this shit to your door. What did Coach say about it?"

"Just that as far as he's concerned, it's hearsay. As long as we're not fooling around at work, and we tell him if it does develop into a relationship, he's happy to tell management he investigated and found the claims were unfounded."

I was acutely aware of the passing of time as Gage dropped onto a stool and scrubbed a hand over his hair.

"That's good, right? You're not in trouble for anything?"

"No, I'm not in trouble. But it isn't going to look good if we arrive late to work in the same car. I'm going to head out now, all right? I'll see you there?"

He seemed to be deep in thought as I stepped out his door and headed back to my car.

The drive into work went faster than expected, and as I strode through the door of the clubhouse, trying not to care that I was still in the clothes from the day before, Coach Byers called out from his office. I changed direction and pulled up short in his doorway. Beside his desk was a tall, willowy girl with blonde hair and eyes the same shade of blue as the man behind the desk.

"How is he?" Coach Byers asked, instead of addressing the woman-shaped elephant in the room.

"He's on his way in. He said he'd play today."

Coach dipped his head in approval.

"He's entitled to time off, but I won't lie and say I don't want him here. He's a good kid."

The woman beside him shuffled from foot to foot.

"Oh, right. Cami Morales, meet my daughter, Maddison. She's going to be helping out around here for the next few weeks. If you need an extra set of hands, she's your girl."

Maddison lifted a hand in an awkward wave and looked back at her father. There was an odd tension between them, but I already had enough on my mind without delving into the head coach's family affairs.

"Would you like to come and watch us run some drills?" I asked instead.

"Yes." She was halfway across the room before the word left her mouth.

"Thanks for the save," she whispered as soon as we were clear of the office. "I love him dearly, but I'm fairly sure if it were legal to chain me to the desk, he'd do it and say he was 'keeping me out of trouble.'" She sketched air quotes with a derisive smile.

Behind us, the double doors clicked open, and a huddled form slipped in.

"Is that Gage Wilson?"

"Ahh, yeah. It is."

"Cool. Hey, don't you hold the record for fastest pitch from, like, ten years ago?"

Maddison—or Maddie, as she asked me to call her—turned out to be a massive fan of women's sports.

"I played in college, but I was never going to be as good as you were. Definitely not now that I've dropped out. I think Dad was on his way to having a coronary before you walked in, so thanks for the save, I guess."

We met the team in the media room and led them down to the gym for pregame conditioning with the help of the trainers.

A stir at the back of the room told me when Gage arrived.

"The prodigal son returns!" Bates yelled from the leg press machine as Bailey jumped down from the pull-up bar and jogged over to slap him on the back.

"You missed me?" Gage asked with a slightly forced grin. The grief was still so visible to me, but his teammates just seemed happy to see him back where he belonged.

"Is that Smith Warren?" Maddie asked, eyeing the huge batter who had entered the room behind Gage. I assumed he'd taken a moment to get the update to avoid Gage having to repeat his news to ad-nauseum.

"I'll introduce you to everyone later and let you know the ones you have to watch. They're all pretty good guys, but they're still guys."

Maddie chuckled. "I get that."

"Hey, if you're going to be around for a while, I have some friends you should meet. You'll love them."

Everyone needed a support system—the last day had been a great reminder of that—and I got the sense that Maddie might not have all that many people in her corner.

"I'd like that. Although I'm going to need to find a place to live."

I grimaced, remembering how much I'd hated house

hunting when I first moved to Chicago. I'd ended up letting Christian take control.

He'd loved it.

As the excitement passed and the players settled into their pregame workouts, Gage caught my eye and smiled.

Ugh, maybe fruitcake wasn't so bad after all.

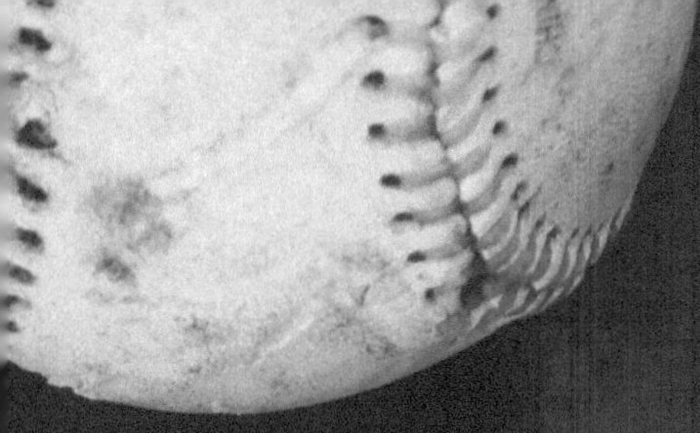

CHAPTER EIGHTEEN

Cami

Over the next few weeks, we somehow settled into an odd rhythm. On nights that we had an early start the following day, Gage, sometimes with Nana in tow, would turn up at my door for dinner and a sleepover. The first time I tripped over Nana on my way to the kitchen, I'd almost broken a toe, but as the days passed, we seemed to have found our own way of moving around each other. She was still terrifyingly big, but Gage was right when he called her zen. Nothing fazed her.

It was early on a Sunday morning, after a big game the night before, when I was woken by the sound of a door slamming.

"Aunt Cami!"

"Shit." I flipped out of bed, landing hard on my hands and knees as Gage let out a groan they could hear at Trident Field.

"Shh, Zara's here." Digging through the mess of

clothing we'd left on the floor, I pulled on the first T-shirt and shorts I found. The hem dropped to my knees, but I had no time to fix the fact I was wearing Gage's clothes as my ten-year-old niece bounded into the bedroom.

"Hey, what are you doing?"

In half a second, she spotted the anomaly in my room.

"Why is he in your bed, Aunt Cami?"

Because I kept accidentally falling into bed with him, even though I swore I wouldn't, and worse, I didn't plan on doing anything to stop it happening again in the near future.

"He was tired, so I let him take a nap."

She eyed him for a long moment, then turned her judgmental gaze on me.

"I thought you hated him?"

"Who told you that?"

"Amber said you wrote it in the chat with her mom. She said that you said you needed help burying a body because he made you mad."

A snort came from beneath the pile of bedding. The asshole wasn't the least bit concerned about my ability to make him disappear if I chose.

"Don't worry, we'll burn the sheets when he leaves."

Zara laughed. "That's silly. Why don't you just wash them?"

This was why I loved this girl. Despite her age, she was forever practical, but she also had a wicked streak that would turn her father gray before we turned forty.

"Good idea, kiddo. Hey, did you see Gage brought his dog around? She's probably in the kitchen."

The promise of doggie love was enough to get Zara out of my bedroom and, hopefully, buy us enough time to get dressed.

"I didn't know she was coming around this morning," I whispered, hustling around the bed and whipping off Gage's shirt so he could put it on. Instead, he caught me around the waist and pulled me down on top of him.

"Good morning," he said, his eyes glowing golden in the morning light.

"Hi."

He lifted his head, pressing a languid kiss against my lips that warmed me up in ways that were not appropriate with my niece in the next room.

"I've come up with a solution," he said with a boyish grin.

"To what?"

"To our dating dilemma."

I frowned and tried to push up off him, but he just tightened his arms around me, keeping me exactly where he wanted me.

I pretended to hate it.

"I wasn't aware we had a dating dilemma. We aren't dating."

"Yes, we are, but we can only date in secret at the moment because we don't want you to lose your job."

I was getting more confused by the minute.

Sure, we'd had a few sleepovers lately, and I really enjoyed what we did during those sleepovers... And maybe some of his clothes had ended up in my drawers, but that was more out of practicality because my house was closer to the stadium.

But we weren't dating...were we?

"But see, that's not going to work for me long-term because I want nothing more than to be able to walk down the street holding your hand, and to let everyone know that the woman I love holds the world record for fastest pitch."

Most of what he'd said felt so overwhelming that I didn't know how to even begin to process it, so I focused on the one thing that stood out to me.

"You want to hold hands?"

"Baby." He took my wrist in a gentle grip and interlaced our fingers. "I'd kill to hold your hand and claim you as mine."

Out in the yard, Zara let out a squeal of delight, to which Nana responded with a single, composed *woof.*

"But I'm a bitch," I said, still struggling with his revelation.

"Yes, sometimes. If you can't tell, I like that side of you. You're also soft, and kinder than you give yourself credit for, and fiercely loyal to anyone you consider your people. Cami, you are the most amazing woman, and anyone would be lucky to get to exist in your orbit. So if what we're doing now is enough for you, then I'll be happy for what attention you'll give me, but if there's a chance we can be more...you'd best believe I'll come up with any plan I can to make it happen."

I studied our linked hands for a long moment, trying to process what he was telling me while a loud voice in my head screamed that he was lying. That this was just a new way to self-sabotage and everything was going to collapse around me.

But maybe that was just it.

The fear of career success made me run from the pros. It was the same reason I'd spoken to Coach Byers while expecting dismissal.

If I were honest with myself, the fear of trying this relationship and having it not work out was crippling, and that was what made me devalue it at every opportunity.

Self-sabotage dressed up as work ethic.

Gage deserved better than that.

“Tell me your plan,” I said, pressing my lips to our joined hands.

“Retirement.”

He said it with such confidence that, at first, I just stared at him, waiting for the punchline.

His glowing grin dimmed as the seconds ticked by without whatever big reaction he was expecting.

“Gage, I just started in this role,” I said carefully, alarm bells ringing in my head.

“Not you. Me.”

“Why would you do that? You can’t do that.”

He slid his free hand down my back, resting it casually on my ass as his stare became contemplative.

“I’m going to be thirty-two in a couple of months, and as much as you think I haven’t been listening to your lectures about injury, I know it’s only a matter of time before something gives. I’ll see out the season, but after that, I want to love you out loud. No more hiding.”

He’d thrown out the L-word twice now, and I wasn’t sure if he even knew he’d said it.

Was I supposed to say it back?

He didn’t seem to be waiting for it.

Did I want to say it back?

“What would you do instead?” I asked as my head started to throb.

“I kinda like the idea of helping out with a certain girl’s baseball team whenever their coach is travelling. Maybe I can volunteer at the retirement village where Gram had her knitting circle. I’m not really interested in going into coaching, but my undergrad was in sports physiology so maybe I could go back to school and become a trainer or something." He shrugged. "The possibilities are actually pretty exciting."

A door slammed, and Zara's voice drifted toward the bedroom. She seemed to be deep in conversation with Nana about squirrels.

"You want to help coach my girls?"

He stretched his arms toward the ceiling, then crossed them behind his head. Despite the stress of his gram's passing, her funeral, and coordinating her last wishes, he seemed at peace.

"I can't think of anything better than training the next generation."

Oh, shit.

My heart swelled as I looked into his golden eyes and saw flashes of how our life could pan out.

Saturday mornings at the field with Zara's team, game nights where he could watch from the stands as the Coyotes fought for the Diamond League title, and the in-between times where neither of us had to pretend to be anyone other than who we were, because who we were together was perfect.

"What's wrong?" he asked, cupping my cheek.

I cursed, rubbing at my watery eyes.

"I just realized I'm stuck with you."

"I'm glad you finally caught up," he said, grinning from ear to ear.

"I love you too, asshole." I tried to push away, feeling far too vulnerable, but he refused to let me go, pulling me into a long kiss that sent warmth all the way to my toes.

Rolling us over, he hovered above me, eyes tracking over my face like he needed to record every detail.

"I love you so much," he whispered.

"Aunt Cami, can we make cookies?" Zara hollered from the general direction of the kitchen.

Pecking a quick kiss on Gage's lips, I squirmed out from beneath him and went hunting for my clothing.

"Raincheck. Last time Zara tried to make cookies alone, she almost burned down half of Christian's kitchen."

As I hustled out of the bedroom to save my house from Zara-related damage, my body felt lighter than it had in a long time. Movement was easier, and the air smelled slightly fresher than before. It wasn't until we were sliding the cookie trays into the oven that I realized what the feeling was.

Happiness.

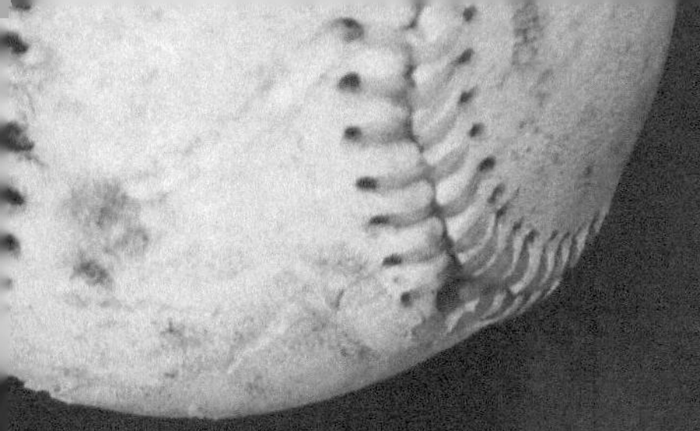

EPILOGUE

Gage

Five months later

TWELVE MONTHS AGO, if someone had asked me where I saw myself today, I would have told them I'd be riding the high of having helped bring home the Diamond League title for the Coyotes and eagerly awaiting pre-season training to do it all again.

I would only have been half right.

Coach Byers had been disappointed to hear of my plan to retire at the end of the season, but weirdly, when Cami mentioned loving fruitcake, he seemed much more open to things.

I wasn't sure what she was talking about, because I knew for a fact she hated golden raisins, but they both seemed happy, so I went with it.

The team was less understanding, and it killed me that I couldn't tell them the whole truth. They'd been my extended family for over a decade. Walking away from them wasn't an easy decision, and I didn't think it was one I would ever have considered unless I knew for a fact I was leaving for something far better.

That far-better thing was clawing at my back as I drove into her in long, hard strokes, making her headboard knock on her wall in an obscene wake-up call for seven in the morning. I hooked her knee over my elbow and changed the angle for her. My eyes crossed as I hit a new depth, and she whimpered.

"Fuck, you feel so good. How are you so perfect?"

In the relatively short time we'd been together, I'd learned her body like I was studying for the most important test of my life. I knew when she needed it hard and rough to get out of her head after a tough day at work, and I knew when she needed me to slow down and worship her with a gentle care she'd never admit she needed. My woman was the strongest person I knew, and the fact she trusted me with her body, her pleasure, and better still, her heart was something I was never going to take for granted.

She arched her back, so close to the edge that I could feel her tighten around me, and I took the opportunity to suck one of her sweet, rosy nipples into my mouth.

"Gage."

I knew what she wanted.

And I'd give it to her.

Dropping her leg, I reached between us and rubbed firm circles on her clit until she came undone with a scream that made me thankful Zara hadn't spent the night.

I loved that kid, but she had a habit of turning up at the most inconvenient times.

And yes, I had my suspicions that Christian was the mastermind behind the inconveniences.

I'd met her brother before we went to the playoffs and

suffered through his threats to dismember and disappear me if I hurt his sister.

Considering his sister was sitting right beside me, making similar threats if he touched me without her express say-so, I wasn't overly worried.

If I hurt Cami, I had no doubt she was more than capable of doing her own dirty work.

I'd even gone for beers with the Engines players a time or two since then, tolerating their inaccurate beliefs about which sport was superior because, other than having poor taste, they were pretty great guys.

I left Cami tangled in the sheets while I threw together coffee and breakfast, then let Nana outside to do her business. As the eggs sizzled in the pan, I took a moment to appreciate that today had finally come.

We were soft-launching our relationship with the team at Smith Warren's post-season cookout.

Or so Cami thought.

I checked my phone and breathed a little easier at the notification that had just come through from Smith. A single thumbs up.

Everything was set.

At eleven thirty, we pulled up in front of a neat little townhouse with a store-bought bowl of potato salad and excitement bubbling through us. Cami looked like a fucking knockout in a pair of tight jeans, a brown knit sweater, and her signature hoop earrings. I couldn't wait to officially show her off.

Inside was surprisingly homey, and I wondered if Smith had hired a designer, or if he had a partner hidden away somewhere that he hadn't mentioned. While he was an amazing player and often organized team-building activities like today, he played his cards close to his chest.

As far as any of us could tell, he lived and breathed baseball without room for anything else.

But he hadn't hesitated to step up when I called.

We wandered through the ground floor, past a huge kitchen setup that looked like it belonged in Gordon Ramsay's house, and found most of the team was already spread out over the back decking.

"Hey!" Chuck called, standing from his crouch beside a built-in firepit to one side of the lawn. "You made it! Too old to play ball, but you'll still turn up for the food. Sounds about right." He cackled at his own joke and jogged up the steps to hug Cami before punching my shoulder.

"You guys arrived together?" he asked, eyeing the point where our shoulders touched. I glanced at Cami.

"Of course they did, dipshit," Smith said, taking the bowl from Cami's hands.

"You haven't noticed them making eyes at each other all year?"

Cami's jaw dropped. I wrapped my arm around her waist. "She couldn't resist me."

As expected, her elbow caught me in the side, and I held her a little tighter.

"Can't get rid of me that easily."

"Asshole."

Pulling out of my grip, she wandered down to the lawn and struck up a conversation with Maddie, Coach Byers's daughter, who looked weirdly at home as she handed out cans of beer and soda.

"You guys make sense, you know," Smith observed, watching the women laugh at something Bailey said to them.

"Yeah?" What time was it? Now that we were here, I just wanted to get things moving.

"She's a little bit mean, and you're a little bit obsessed with her. You're the perfect pair."

I chuckled along with him because he was right.

When I'd first approached him about commandeering this get-together, I'd expected him to be surprised, maybe doubt my sanity, because who would believe someone like Cami would ever look twice at me, but he'd just clapped me on the shoulder and told me he'd guessed it weeks earlier.

Apparently, I hadn't been as subtle as I thought.

"Do you want me to bring out the pastries now?"

My phone buzzed in my pocket.

Showtime.

I nodded to Smith and jogged down the stairs and across the lawn toward my future.

Cami greeted me with a smile as I stepped up beside her, my heart thundering a million miles a minute.

What if she thought this was too soon?

What if she didn't want this at all?

"Aunt Cami!"

"Shhh."

Cami frowned, turning toward the house.

"Zara?"

Shit. Ok. Now or never.

Scrubbing my hands on my jeans, I pulled out the ring I'd slipped into my pocket when she wasn't looking. I'd wanted to buy her the biggest, gaudiest ring I could. Something that was visible to the International Space Station so everyone would know she was mine.

But that wasn't Cami.

So instead, I'd settled for a simple yellow gold band with a perfect-clarity round-cut diamond. Something that, I hoped, she could wear at work without it getting in the way.

As Cami's brother and niece stepped out onto the decking with their closest friends, I dropped to one knee behind her.

Maddie gasped and stepped back, nudging Cami, who turned and froze, her confused frown relaxing in surprise.

"Cami Morales," I started as the other players in the backyard began to crowd around, some murmured in surprise and others shushed them.

Shit. I'd had a speech planned out, but it turned out the nerves I hadn't experienced on the mound since I was a rookie player had decided to make a show, clearing all of the perfectly planned words from my head in favor of running showreels of her turning her back on me.

I cleared my throat and tried again.

"Cami, you are a force of nature. Since you threw that snowball at me for being a petulant idiot, you haven't missed a beat telling me how it really is."

Zara giggled and was hushed by her father.

"You are fierce and kind and everything I could ever ask for in a partner, and I'm going to take a leap here and hope to God that I'm what you need too. We've spent too long hiding, and I'm so excited to let the world know I'm yours. Will you marry me?"

Cami glanced from me, to her family, and around the yard at all the people who had come to be like a surrogate family.

"Say yes, Aunt Cami, then we get to keep Nana."

She laughed and leaned down until her face was inches from mine.

"Yes." Her words coasted across my lips, and joy bubbled through my limbs as I closed the distance between us and took her mouth in a scorching kiss.

Hoots and hollers filled the yard from the players, while Christian grumbled.

Smith stepped out of the house with a heaping tray of danishes, and Cami got first pick of the apple.

We spent the afternoon celebrating with food and friends, and that evening I took her home, marveling at how such a simple ring could look so elevated on the right hand.

It looked like a perfect future.

***

Thank you so much for reading!

If you loved Cami and Gage's story, please consider leaving a review.

Are you up to date in the warrior universe? You can ready Gia and Weston's story, False Start today!

Want to spend some more time getting to know Christian Morales? Keep an eye out for his book, Passing Play, coming soon.

Sign up for TL's newsletter to find out about new books!

Next up in the Diamond Warriors series is Curveball of Desire by Michelle Savage

READ THE DIAMOND WARRIORS SERIES

Unexpected Curveball by Heather Dahlgren

Between Second and Sin by Melissa Filla

Curveballs and Kisses by Kathleen Kelly

Double Play by Annelise Reynolds

Wild Pitch by TL Hamilton

Curveball of Desire by Michelle Savage

Catcher's Interference by A. R. Hall

Breaking the Ladder by Chelle C. Craze

Catching Hearts and Flowers by Jaime Russell

Chasing the Heat by Dawn Sullivan

Catching Feelings by Quinn Ryder

Pickle Trap by Maria Vickers

Fair Catch by Amy Stephens

ALSO BY TL HAMILTON

M/F Sports Romance

The Perfect Stroke

Split - Kane & Darcy Pt 1

Shatter - Kane & Darcy Pt 2

Shock - Evie & Xavier

Fox Academy

Kicking it with the Winger Oscar & Mia

Austin Aces Hockey Club

Slapshot - Cian & Blair

Warrior Sports League

False Start - Weston & Gia

Wild Pitch - Cami & Gage

Passing Play - Christian & Marina

M/F Military Romantic Suspense

At All Costs

Target Me

Heal Me

Contemporary RH

The One For Us

The not so secret life of a wish maker

Where in the world (Stand alone in 'The One For Us' universe)

Goldenfire Records

Not With the Band

Zodiac Assassins

The book of Gemini

Paranormal RH

Moon Dust Library/ Silver Springs Library Standalones

Moonlit Alexandrite

Moonlit Alexandrite: Crafty Seductions

Jewels Cafe: Jacinth

The Cursed Coven of Spells Hollow

Warrior Witch (co write with Katherine Isaac)

ABOUT THE AUTHOR

TL Hamilton hails from Melbourne, Australia, where she lives with her hubby, two (not so) little boys, and menagerie of animals.

The consummate daydreamer, TL writes all over the romance spectrum from romcom right through to the dark, gritty, hold onto your seats drama. Regardless of the story, you can guarantee you'll find relatable characters and steamy bedroom times between the covers of her books.

Reviews are the life blood of indie authors, so if you read her work and enjoy it, please consider leaving a review in exchange for her everlasting adoration.

Come and join the fun in her reader group on Facebook

www.tlhamiltonauthor.com

ACKNOWLEDGMENTS

Whenever I start writing a story, there is me, and there are the characters. Some are loud and demanding, while others are reserved and need coaxing out.

When they first land on the page, I have no idea whether their story is something that people will enjoy, or utter nonsense. This is the point when I add Jamie, my alpha reader to the document.

Jamie, from pointing out when I fall into soccer references because I don't know the baseball equivalent to whipping me into shape when I abandon the story, you are an amazing support without whom I would be lost. Thank you for being there with me every step of the way.

To my editor, Katie, thank you for your patience and flexibility when the characters decide to change things up. I can't wait to do this all again with you in a few months.

To my author friends both at home and overseas, thank you for being there to support me through the lows of imposter syndrome, and highs of signings and panel speaking opportunities with laughs, lunches and smiles.

A huge thank you to my cover designer, Clarise Tan, whose work has been impeccable with these Warrior Sports League books (I can't wait to show everyone the next one!)

Another huge thank you has to go to Lindee Robinson for the stunning cover photo.

To my fellow authors in the warrior Sports League

world, thank you for making this such a fun and enjoyable experience. Let's do it again soon!

To my friends and family for letting me rant about my characters, and especially my husband for managing the house when I'm on deadline and writing for absurd lengths of time, thank you.

And lastly, to you, the reader.

Without you I'm shouting into a void and arguing with the voices in my head, so thank you for picking up this book and taking a chance on Cami and Gage's little story.

I hope they gave you what you were looking for.

See you in the next book,

TL

www.ingramcontent.com/pod-product-compliance
Lightning Source LLC
LaVergne TN
LVHW091149080826
845145LV00008B/2304